I'll See You In My Dreams

I'll See You In My Dreams

ILENE COOPER

Viking

VIKING

Published by the Penguin Group

Penguin Putnam Inc., 375 Hudson Street, New York, New York 10014, U.S.A.

Penguin Books Ltd, 27 Wrights Lane, London W8 5TZ, England

Penguin Books Australia Ltd, Ringwood, Victoria, Australia

Penguin Books Canada Ltd, 10 Alcorn Avenue, Toronto, Ontario, Canada M4V 3B2

Penguin Books (N.Z.) Ltd, 182–190 Wairau Road, Auckland 10, New Zealand

Penguin Books Ltd, Registered Offices: Harmondsworth, Middlesex, England

First published in 1997 by Viking, a member of Penguin Putnam Inc.

1 3 5 7 9 10 8 6 4 2

LIBRARY OF CONGRESS CATALOGING-IN-PUBLICATION DATA

Cooper, Ilene.

I'll see you in my dreams / by Ilene Cooper.

p. cm.

Summary : Karen's dreams, which years ago foretold the death of her father, are now
warning her of another impending tragedy.

ISBN 0-670-86322-X (hc)

[1. Dreams—Fiction. 2. Extrasensory perception—Fiction.]

I. Title.

PZ7.C7856I1 1997 [Fic]—dc21 96-54049 CIP AC

Printed in U.S.A.

Set in New Caledonia

Where was the bus? Karen hugged her arms, rubbing up and down against her flannel shirt. September and it felt more like Halloween. She should have worn a jacket, but the one her mother had brought home looked like something out of the J. Crew catalog. Not her style.

She glanced toward the corner, but instead of the big yellow school bus she was looking for, Karen saw *him*. Ambling down the street, as if he had all the time in the world, was the new guy. He had been at the bus stop the first day of school, and he showed up every once in a while since then, appearing out of one of the big houses at the edge of the ravine. How did he get to school the other days? Did he drive? Karen supposed he could be sixteen, although he looked more like a fifteen-year-old sophomore, like her. He crossed the street toward her, and Karen averted her head.

✦   ✦   ✦

Mark took his place on the corner. He was careful not to get too close to the girl, who always kept the mailbox between them like a bodyguard. Mark pretended she wasn't there and wondered why she was such a snob. He had said hello to her that first day. He was almost sure he had. Even if he hadn't, would it have killed her to say good morning to him? After all, he was the one who was new at West Ridge High. Not that he needed her. He was doing all right in the friend department. Still, a smile would be nice.

Instead, she looked as if he scared her to death.

CHAPTER 1

Karen made her way to the back of the bus. She barely glanced at her fellow riders, a jabbering, jostling group. There was only one person Karen was looking for, and she knew exactly where she'd find her. In the last row, huddled in the corner, was a sleeping Mimi Post. Karen made a freshman boy move over so that she had a patch of seat next to her friend.

Karen gave her the elbow. "Wake up," she hissed.

But Mimi just shifted herself and didn't open an eye.

How could Mimi sleep so hard on a bus? Karen wondered. She could hardly get a decent night's sleep at home in her own bed, and here was Mimi beatifically snoozing away on a school bus through a wall of noise.

"You're snoring." Karen tried again. "You're drooling for the whole school to see."

Mimi opened one eye, then dragged her manicured fingers along her chin. "I am not."

"No, you're not," Karen conceded. "But you might have been." She looked down at her own hands. Fingernails bitten down to the quick.

"So, what's up?" Mimi asked, stifling a yawn.

"That boy was at the bus stop again," Karen said, glancing over to the front of the bus where he was chatting with Jenny Cullen, the queen of the junior class.

"He's got a name," Mimi informed her. "It's Mark. Mark Kennedy."

"How did you find out?" Karen asked, in what she hoped was a nonchalant voice.

But, as usual, Mimi was on to her. "How did you find out?" Mimi repeated mockingly. "I did what you should have done. I asked someone."

"I've told you, Mimi, he's not my type."

"Then why do you keep dreaming about him?" Mimi asked slyly.

Karen cursed herself for ever telling Mimi that she had been dreaming about the boy—Mark, if that's what his name was. At least she had never told Mimi exactly what the dreams were about. That would start a conversation that would never end.

"Did you dream about him last night?" Mimi asked.

"No," Karen lied.

"Dreams are very significant," Mimi said. She began

to rummage around in her backpack and pulled out a slightly tattered paperback. "I saw this in a used bookstore by my house. It was only fifty cents, so I bought it for you."

"*The Secret World of Dreams,*" Karen read aloud. "So what am I supposed to do with it?"

"Well, excuse me," Mimi said huffily. "I thought it might interest you."

Mimi must really be offended, Karen thought. Her dimples had disappeared. "You're right." Karen made her tone placating. "I should try and figure out what my dreams mean."

If only Mimi knew the half of it. Karen rubbed her finger along the spine of the book. Dreams were a secret world, all right, a world that sometimes felt more real to her than the universe of school and family that she inhabited during her waking hours. Shrouded, dark, this was a place where events moved like quicksilver. The dreams she held on to were the ones that came true.

But Karen didn't want to think about that now. She pasted a smile on her face and said to Mimi, "That's a great sweater."

Mimi let herself be distracted. "My stepmother sent it to me. She got it at one of those vintage clothing stores in Manhattan." Picking a fuzz ball off the pink mohair sweater, she added, "It's real sixties."

How lucky could you get? A stepparent with a sense of style. Karen's own stepfather was perfectly boring. So boring, he was an insurance salesman. Not that Don was a bad guy or anything. The ten-year-old Karen had been glad when her widowed mother remarried, mostly because her mother had finally stopped crying. Karen supposed her parents were nice enough, but they sure weren't going to win any hipness awards.

"You always look so great," Karen said wistfully.

Mimi laughed. "Not according to the style set at West Ridge High. It's preppie all the way."

"You have your own style," Karen argued. "Besides, you've got that great curly hair, and those blue eyes."

"You have blue eyes," Mimi pointed out.

"It's not the same," Karen muttered. And it wasn't. Mimi's eyes were a pretty blue. Karen's were the color of jeans that had been through the washer once too often, and her brown hair just hung at her shoulders.

"We'll do a makeover on you," Mimi said eagerly. "I've been begging you to let me have a go at it since the summer."

It was true. Karen and Mimi had had a few classes together last year, but they'd only became friends during the summer. They kept running into each other at the park where they took the kids they were babysitting. Almost from the first, Mimi was suggesting a new hairdo or shopping trips.

Mimi was an independent spirit. There were other kids she hung around with, but she was equally happy to be on her own. For Karen, having a friend was something new. Oh, there had been girls she'd played with when she was younger, but after her father died, Karen had tended to keep to herself. Her mother, who was always pushing her to have friends over, thought that it was her dad's death that had traumatized Karen. She was partially right. Karen hadn't felt like letting people get close to her since her father's accident, but that wasn't the main reason she was so standoffish. It was the dreams that had made her feel different from other girls her age. Different from everyone really. How many people had dreams that came true?

"You're going to be hot," Mimi continued happily. "We're finally going to do it. You'll see then."

Karen sighed. She didn't really like change. She preferred things to be predictable, even if that meant boring, but Mimi had that determined glint in her eye. *Oh why not?* Karen thought to herself.

The bus came to a halt in front of West Ridge High. It was a funny-looking building, mostly red brick and as solid as a prison. But a wing had been added twenty or so years ago that was low-slung and modern. The whole thing looked odd and out of whack. Just the way Karen figured she was going to look after Mimi got done with her.

Mark was one of the first kids off the bus. He could hang back, he supposed, and walk with Jenny and the others, but he had had enough of trying to make chitchat. He knew he should be grateful that he had gotten in with the in-crowd so fast, but really, it was only because they fell for his scam.

He was good looking. It always gave him a head start on making friends. And he was a fast learner. His family had moved around a lot, and instinctively he seemed to be able to look around, figure out which kids were the right kids, and copy their style of talk and dress. All this in record time. When his family lived in L.A., Mark had become a surfer type. Last semester, at a private school on Manhattan's Upper East Side, he had played the part of the intellectual. Now, here in West Ridge, an hour and a half from New York City, he was the king of suburbia, preppie version. He was anybody the fans wanted him to be.

Mark watched as the girl from the bus stop and her friend hurried past him. He wished he knew her name, although he wasn't sure why. One thing was certain, he couldn't ask anyone. She was not the right type to be inquiring about. It was pretty easy to separate the outs from the ins.

Still, she interested him. He kept thinking that one day he would just talk to her at the bus stop. It shouldn't be that hard to say hi. After all, he knew how to do it with everyone else.

As they walked past Mark, Mimi glanced at him over her shoulder.

"Quit looking," Karen hissed.

"Please, he's lost in space. He doesn't even know we're here."

Karen supposed that was true. Nevertheless, she didn't

want to risk him looking up and catching Mimi's interested glance.

Karen left Mimi at her locker and went to homeroom. Mrs. Aikman, her homeroom teacher, was writing at her desk. Karen liked Mrs. Aikman a lot. She had had her for homeroom last year, and they had struck up a friendship. One of the things Karen had been looking forward to in sophomore year was taking Mrs. Aikman's English class, where it was said that Shakespeare became not only intelligible but occasionally awesome. Instead, she had been placed in Mr. Cochran's English class. A fidgety guy who mumbled, Mr. Cochran had trouble keeping control of his class. The boys kept making rude, gassy noises whenever he turned to write on the blackboard.

Mrs. Aikman looked up and caught Karen's eye. "Karen, could you come here for a moment?"

Karen put down her books and walked over to Mrs. Aikman's desk.

Mrs. Aikman smiled at her. "Are you feeling adaptable today?"

"Do I have to?"

"I'm afraid so. I have a schedule change for you."

"But we've been in school for almost three weeks," Karen replied, dismayed.

"Mr. Cochran has resigned."

"You mean he's leaving?"

"I mean he's left."

"Probably for the best," Karen murmured.

Mrs. Aiken didn't respond, but a knowing smile played around her lips. "In any case, the office is frantically trying to place his students in other classes. Since you have study hall last period, you've been moved to my English class, and you'll have a study fourth period. Any problem with that?"

"It's fine," Karen said. "I wanted to be in your class anyway," she added shyly.

"Then it's settled. I'll tell the office to make the change. Come to my class in room 125. I hope I live up to your expectations."

Karen didn't know how to answer that, so she just nodded and went back to her desk. No more Cochran, and Mrs. Aikman to boot. It put Karen in a good mood for the rest of the day.

At two o' clock, she walked into English class and took a seat toward the back of the room. She had forgotten to ask Mrs. Aikman how far her class had progressed with *Romeo and Juliet,* which was the first reading assignment on the sophomore syllabus. Mr. Cochran hadn't gotten very far. It was hard to talk about young love when it seemed like almost every boy in the class had gas. Mr. Cochran had spent a lot of time discussing Shakespeare's England.

Karen opened her paperback *Romeo and Juliet* and began reading it. She never had any problems with her English classes. Even if she was behind in the work, she'd be able to make it up.

As she read, Karen was aware that someone had taken

the seat next to her, but she didn't look up. When the bell rang, she closed her book, and suddenly felt as though she were a pin, and a magnet was across the aisle, drawing her to face it. She followed the pull and looked at the boy across from her. Before she could stop herself, Karen said, "Hello, Mark."

CHAPTER 2

Mark felt himself flush, but he didn't know if it was from embarrassment or relief. She knew his name. Then immediately he wondered how long she had known it.

"Hi," he managed and wondered how to ask her name. But Mrs. Aikman was already standing in front of her desk, talking about the Montagues and the Capulets, so he shrugged slightly and turned his attention to the front of the room.

Idiot! Karen berated herself. *Now, he's going to think I'm interested or something. That I've been asking around about him.* She wanted to glance over and gauge his reaction, but she restrained herself. Resolutely, she tried to focus in on what Mrs. Aikman was saying, but it was too hard to pay attention.

The feeling she had had when he walked into the room, that magnet effect, was the familiar draw she had felt whenever he walked into her dreams. And the dreams had been going on for months, even though the first time she had seen him in real life had been at the bus stop on the day school started.

Don't think about it, she told herself desperately. She had spent a lot of time lately trying to forget her dreams, and occasionally she was successful.

"Karen . . ."

Karen looked up at the sound of Mrs. Aikman speaking her name.

"I was just asking how far in the play Mr. Cochran had gotten."

The question was like a splash of cold water, bringing Karen back into the world of desks, books, and doodling students. "Actually, we hadn't started reading it yet."

Fred Ellenbogan, another transfer from Cochran's class added, smiling slightly, "The class was noisy, very hard to concentrate in."

There were a few suppressed giggles from other transferees.

Mrs. Aikman had been a teacher long enough to know something was up, and was smart enough to know she didn't want to find out what. "Well, I'm sorry to say that you're behind. We're well into the second act, which I'd like you to have finished by Friday." She looked around the room. "Mark, can you bring the newcomers up to speed?"

Mark didn't mind. This was the kind of thing he did best. He leaned back in his chair and told the story of the feuding families, and how Romeo and Juliet had met. Karen wondered if he had ever considered going into acting.

"Thank you, Mark," Mrs. Aikman said and then continued with the class. It was a testament to Mrs. Aikman's teaching ability that Karen was able to turn her attention from the romance she was fantasizing about in her mind to the one on the pages of her textbook.

When the bell rang, Karen hurriedly gathered her books. Mark moved a little more slowly. The room was emptying. Even Mrs. Aikman was gone.

As Karen tried to move by him, Mark's voice stopped her. "Uh, Karen . . ." That's what Mrs. Aikman had called her.

"Yes?" Karen asked warily.

"I've taken a lot of notes on *Romeo and Juliet*. Do you want to borrow them?"

It was a perfect opening, Karen knew that. But all her dreams got mixed up with the moment. Sounding abrupt, she said, "Thanks, but I don't think I'll need them."

Mark tried to cover his surprise. "Whatever," he replied stiffly. He grabbed his things and headed outside. When he arrived on the steps, he melted into the group that was already hanging out there. Jenny Cullen was wearing her cheerleader sweater over a pair of jeans, which was strictly against the rules, but she looked great in the outfit anyway.

"We're going to the Barn," she twinkled up at him. "Want to come with?"

Still smarting from Karen's brush-off, he nodded. He didn't have anything better to do.

Karen passed the group on her way to the bus. None of them noticed her, not even Mark. She looked at Mark as she walked by. Why hadn't she just accepted his offer of the notes? It wouldn't have been such a big deal. Now it was too late, and she had probably blown it for good. Karen sighed. He was so clearly one of them. She didn't see how she could ever be a part of that world, not even in her dreams.

It was a relief to walk into her house, to be anywhere but school. Her mother wasn't home yet from her job at the bank. But her stepsister, Gwen, was in front of the television watching a talk show.

"No television until you've done your homework," Karen reminded her.

Gwen barely looked up. "This is about teenage girls who dress too old for their age."

Karen glanced at the television set. "They look like sluts," she said bluntly.

"The one with the blond hair is thirteen," Gwen informed her. "Only a year older than me."

"Don't get any ideas."

Gwen had come to live with them a couple of years

ago, when her own mother had gone back to school and decided that homework and a young daughter were too much to handle. Her mother had graduated and was a social worker now, but Gwen was comfortable in West Ridge and had made a fuss about returning to Boston where her mother lived. Finally it was decided that Gwen would stay with her dad, until it was time to go to high school, anyway.

It had been a shock when Gwen moved in. Of course, she had been visiting since Don and Karen's mother started dating, but that wasn't the same as having her underfoot all the time. At first, Gwen's presence had annoyed Karen, who appreciated the benefits that came with being an only child, but eventually she had gotten used to having a full-time sister. Gwen had a couple of things going for her, Karen had learned. She thought the sun rose and set on Karen, and, at least when she was younger, Gwen had been a willing little slave, ready to run and fetch at Karen's command. Lately, though, she wasn't quite so pliable and didn't seem to hold Karen in such high esteem. *Well, why should Gwen be different from everyone else?* Karen thought.

Gwen hadn't made a move to turn off the television. "What about the homework?" Karen asked.

"I don't have any." Gwen rolled over to look at her. A commercial had come on. "What's wrong?"

"Why do you think anything's wrong?"

"You look kind of mopey."

"I'm just tired. I haven't been sleeping too well lately."

Gwen nodded. "I hear you walking around at night."

"You do?" Karen asked with surprise. She'd assumed that her nocturnal roamings were unnoticed. When her dreams disrupted her sleep, she often headed down to the kitchen to have a cup of microwave hot chocolate. But no one ever came down to join her.

"Do you have bad dreams?" Gwen asked, looking at her owlishly through her glasses.

"I have dreams. They're not bad, exactly."

"So what are they?"

Karen smiled tightly. "Realistic."

"What are they about?"

Before Karen could answer, her mother walked into the room. Mrs. Lewis was a neater version of her daughter. The same slim build and brown lanky hair, but her blouse was neatly tucked in her skirt, and her hair was held in place by a tortoise-shell headband.

"Hi, Mom," Karen greeted her.

"Hi, Barbara," Gwen said, before turning back to the TV.

Names were a funny thing in their house, emblematic of loose connections. To start with, everybody but Karen was a Lewis; Karen had insisted on keeping her father's last name, Genovese. She had been about eleven when Don asked her if she would like him to adopt her, and she had promptly said no. It seemed disloyal to her father somehow. Despite her thumbs-down on the adoption, she still called Don "Dad" most of the time at home, and always when she was in public. She didn't want people to know that she didn't have a father, and Don was better than nothing. Gwen, on the other hand, always called her stepmother by her first name, Barbara. Obviously, she felt the title Mom was already taken, even if the woman it belonged to was a little haphazard at her job.

Mrs. Lewis picked the remote control off the couch and clicked it, leaving Gwen looking bewildered at a black screen for a second or two before she realized what had happened.

"Hey." She sat up outraged.

"Gwen, you know what I think of those shows. Garbage."

Gwen pursed her lips and didn't bother to argue back. It was hard to make a case for TV talk shows.

Karen, feeling a little big sisterly, mildly defended Gwen. "She doesn't have any homework,"

"Good, then she can go outside and ride her bike." Gwen had a tendency to be on the chunky side, so Mrs. Lewis was always ready with a suggestion for physical activity.

"It's fre-e-e-zing," Gwen protested.

Both Karen and Mrs. Lewis had to smile at that. "Well, it's chilly," Mrs. Lewis conceded, "but freezing is pushing it."

Gwen got up. "If I can't watch television, can I go to my room and read?"

Mrs. Lewis nodded. When Gwen was out of earshot,

she said, "It's hard to tell a child she shouldn't be reading, but I wish she'd move around a little more. I've tried to sign her up for ballet, ice skating, even horseback riding, but she just says no, no, no."

Karen shrugged. "So she's not athletic. Her grades are great and she's got lots of friends."

"That is important," Mrs. Lewis said quietly.

Karen knew where this was going. "Oh, goody, now we're going to talk about me."

"It's just that . . ."

"Mom, I've got a friend. What do you call Mimi?"

Mrs. Lewis pursed her lips.

"Well, I'm sorry she doesn't meet with your approval, but Mimi happens to be very nice."

"I'm sure she's nice. She just doesn't seem like your type."

"Beggars can't be choosers," Karen said bitterly. What did her mother want from her? She was never going to be one of those stupid cheerleader types like Jenny Cullen. Wasn't that clear by now?

"When I was your age, I had a whole circle of nice friends."

"Lucky you," Karen muttered and turned to follow Gwen upstairs.

Her mother's words stopped her. "You have a letter."

For the first time, Karen noticed the mail in her mother's hand. "Who's it from?"

"Your grandmother."

"Nana?" That was what she called her mom's mother.

"No, it's from your Grandmother Genovese."

Now Karen was really surprised. "Where is she?"

"The postmark says New York."

Karen took the letter. "It's been a long time since I heard from her." Her father's mother was rarely in the country. For a while, she had lived in London, then she spent a year in Rome. Even when she was back in her apartment in Manhattan, she wasn't much for keeping in touch.

Mrs. Lewis stood by expectantly, but Karen had no intention of reading the letter in front of her mother. "I'll read it later," she said, slipping it into her shirt pocket.

"Whatever you want." Mrs. Lewis shrugged. She knew a power play when she saw one. "I'm not going to start dinner for a while, so why don't you get some homework done."

Karen grabbed her books and headed upstairs. She had never really liked their old barn of a house, but she had been grateful for its size when Gwen arrived. At least she didn't have to share a room. Gwen's style of decorating consisted of putting up pictures of dogs and kittens on every spare inch of wall.

Mrs. Lewis had done the decorating on Karen's room when they first moved in, and the operative word was girlish. Tiny bouquets of roses dotted the wallpaper, and the curtains were white and lacy. It was not at all what Karen would have chosen for herself now. But she was unsure of what she did like, and at least this was familiar and restful.

Throwing her books on the old wooden desk that her mother called an almost-antique, Karen settled herself on the bed. She pulled the letter out of her pocket, ripped the envelope open and began reading.

Dear Karen,

I won't even bother with apologies for not writing more. It's not a very nice thing to admit about oneself (or to oneself for that matter), but I am the person for whom the saying "Out of sight, out of mind" was coined. My travels have taken me far from my family, and as you well know, I have been away emotionally as well as physically.

Nevertheless, I am back now, and expect to be in New York for the foreseeable future. It seems to me that we have much to talk about and finally we have the time to explore the many questions you must have about your father's side of the family. You have my telephone number. Please call soon so that we can arrange a visit. My regards to your mother and her husband.

It was signed *Vivian Genovese*.

Karen was tempted to throw the letter in the garbage. "Vivian Genovese," she said aloud in a snooty voice. Grandma, even Grandmother would have seemed a little friendlier. But why should she expect friendly from a woman whom she barely saw?

Still, Karen thought, rolling over, and staring out the window, her grandmother had dangled a tempting piece of bait. She did want to talk about her father, and who better to talk to than his own mother?

It wasn't that Barbara Lewis avoided the topic of her first husband. She brought his name easily enough into the conversation when it was appropriate, and whenever she found a photo or some memento, she made sure to show it to Karen. But from the time her mother had married Don, Karen had clearly gotten the message that Nicholas Genovese was the past and Don Lewis was the future. Karen guessed she couldn't blame her mother for wanting to put her dad on a shelf and only dust him off periodically. Remembering had to be painful, especially considering how suddenly Nick Genovese had died. Suddenly, that is, for everyone but Karen.

Determinedly, Karen turned away from the window and sat down at her desk. Geometry called. Karen got good grades, but she wasn't a natural student like Gwen, especially when it came to math. Karen didn't mind studying hard. She had learned over the years that hitting the books was a good antidote to what ailed her. Isosceles triangles, precise and unequivocal, would make a pleasant change from dreams, long-lost grandmothers, even Mark.

When her mother called up the stairs that dinner was ready, Karen wasn't even sure how long she had been studying. Reluctantly, she closed her book.

"Everything's done," Karen said with surprise as she came into the kitchen, where the table was even set.

"I helped," Gwen said unenthusiastically, folding one final napkin.

Mrs. Lewis gave Karen a glance. Apparently, if she couldn't get Gwen on her bike, she could at least get her moving around the kitchen. "You can clean up," she told Karen.

Mr. Lewis, yawning from his daily after-work nap, joined the rest of the family. "What's for dinner?"

"Fish," Mrs. Lewis responded.

Mr. Lewis wrinkled his nose. "I should have guessed." Gwen got her girth from him, and lately, Mrs. Lewis was trying to cut his calories by serving lots of fish and vegetables. He took the smallest piece on the platter.

Mrs. Lewis tried to make dinner a time when the family got together and shared the news of the day, but it didn't work very well. Gwen answered questions about her English test in monosyllables, and Don wasn't much more forthcoming about his business trip to New Jersey.

Finally, Mrs. Lewis said in voice calculatedly nonchalant, "Karen got a letter from Nick's mother today."

"Really," Mr. Lewis replied as he pushed his fish around his plate. "It's been a while since we've heard from her. What did Vivian have to say?"

The ploy was clear, but Karen didn't see any way out. Mrs. Lewis knew Karen wouldn't be rude to Don or just refuse to answer his question. "She asked me to come and visit her in Manhattan."

"So, she's back in the city," Don said. "Well, are you going?"

Karen glanced over at her mother, who was obviously surprised by the invitation. With a small smile of satisfaction, she replied, "Why, yes. Yes I am."

CHAPTER 3

Night. Sleep time. Dream time. Karen put it off as long as possible every night. Because she wasn't that interested in television—unlike Gwen—she was allowed a small black-and-white television in her room. So at night, after everyone was asleep, Karen would turn on the set very low, watch the late-night comedians, and force herself to keep her eyes open.

Tonight though, she put on her old flannel pajamas, added a pair of heavy socks to warm her freezing feet, and got under the covers with Mimi's dream book.

Thumbing through it, she saw a chapter about how to remember your dreams. *That's the last thing I need*, she thought. *I already remember too much about them.*

Studding the pages were names like Freud and Jung, who had helped their patients interpret their dreams, and a list of what various items could possibly symbolize. She glanced through it, but nothing seemed to apply to her dreams, which told long stories that wove themselves into her heart.

Tossing the book down on her floor, Karen stared at the ceiling and thought about last summer when the dreams had started up again. When the first one came, she had been mad and scared. She had thought that sort of dream was in the past.

The dreams had begun when she was quite young, maybe five or so. She had known right away they were different from other dreams, the soft, out-of-focus kind. These dreams were crisp and realistic, and something in them always came true. The first one she remembered was about her cat, Whiskers. In the dream, Whiskers was gone. She had looked everywhere, becoming increasingly frantic, but she couldn't find him anywhere. Karen woke up crying, and even as her dad held her in his arms and told her it was only a dream, she knew that it was something more. For a while, she watched Whiskers like a hawk, but after a couple of days, she grew careless with her surveillance, and soon after, Whiskers got out of the house and never came back. Karen had been angry with herself because she hadn't been able to keep her cat safe.

The next dream had been about breaking an expensive porcelain doll Vivian had sent her from Germany. As soon as she had the dream, she tried to avoid the doll; she even lied and said she didn't want to play with it anymore, satisfied when her mother put it on a shelf.

But one day when she was tossing a ball in her room, it had bounced against the shelf, and the doll fell off. Karen had once again been distraught, which surprised her mother. "I thought you didn't even like that doll."

Karen had tried to explain about her dream, but perhaps she was too young to really make herself understood. Her mother had just shrugged it off.

Had her mother paid more attention when Karen had dreamed of her father's death? Karen didn't remember. She tried very hard to remember as little as possible about those days and the dreams that preceded her father's accident. And after so many years, she had succeeded. Most of the details were gone. But not all of them.

After her father died, there'd been long periods of time, to her blessed relief, when the dreams had come only sporadically. There were still the everyday kind of dreams of course, but only once in a while did Karen have dreams or a series of dreams that were predictions of events to come.

That had changed last July. Karen remembered it especially because the first of the Mark dreams came the night after Mimi's birthday party. When she awoke the next morning, feeling exhausted and with her stomach rumbling, Karen had tried to persuade herself she had eaten too much ice cream and cake. But she wasn't a little kid who didn't know when to stop stuffing herself. The odd, disoriented feeling had come with the pictures she saw in her sleep.

The dream had started like the ones in her past. It didn't seem like a dream at all. As in the dreams of her childhood, everything seemed so real, except that the colors were somehow brighter than they were in life, burnished to a shine. In that July dream, Karen had been walking beside a river that looked like it was full of diamonds, but then she realized that it was only the sun shining on the water. Suddenly, the setting changed. Karen was plunked down in the middle of the West Ridge lunchroom, with its greasy cafeteria smells and the students creating a din.

Karen was alone in this sea of diners. That was real enough. Before Mimi, she had often sat by herself. She was reading a book and eating her sandwich when the first magnetic pull came. Karen looked up and she saw him. The boy that she now knew was Mark was standing alone in the doorway, and Karen wanted to run to him and join him. Then she felt a sinking sensation in the pit of her stomach. There was some trouble that came with this boy.

She got up and hurried toward him anyway, but she woke up before she got there.

That had been the start of the dreams that had come first weekly, then every few days. This was the longest series of dreams that Karen had ever had, and that fact alone scared her.

The setting for the dreams was usually school. There were always other kids around, sometimes dressed in odd costumes, but it never seemed to bother her in the dreams that clowns and pirates walked the halls of West Ridge High. She was with Mark in the dreams now, and she couldn't deny that she was attracted to him. But he barely looked at her, which made Karen mad, because there was something she needed to tell him. If only she knew what it was.

Once, he asked her, "What do you want?"

"I . . . I . . ." The words seemed so close, but just out of reach.

He got mad at her. "Then leave me alone."

"I can't."

Through her weeks of summer dreaming, Karen's only solace was that whoever this boy was, he was only a figment of her nighttime imagination. Until he showed up at the bus stop on the first day of school.

In retrospect, Karen was amazed she hadn't sensed him coming. She always knew when he was about to appear in her dreams. But on that first day, she had only been worried about her hair, which she hadn't had time to finish drying, because the dryer was on the fritz. Patches of hair were plastered against her head like wet spaghetti, and Karen wondered if she shouldn't just go home and pretend school started tomorrow.

She had just pulled her mirror out of her knapsack for a quick glance, when she saw him approaching. Clutching the mirror so hard her fingers hurt, Karen tried to tell herself that this boy just looked like the one in her dreams, but as he got closer, there was no mistaking his appearance for mere resemblance. It was him.

Now, she couldn't remember what she had done when he finally stood beside her. Maybe she had acknowledged his tentative hello, but perhaps she'd just turned away until the bus arrived, which was mercifully soon. In the days after that, she had tried to ignore him both in her dreams and at the bus stop, failing miserably on both accounts.

A knock at the door interrupted Karen's musings. Instinctively, she tucked the dream book she was still holding under the covers. Karen was surprised to see her mother come in. Mrs. Lewis was notorious for turning in early.

"I couldn't sleep," Mrs. Lewis said, as she stood at the door, bundled up in a chenille robe and wearing the silly bunny-head slippers Gwen had given her for Christmas several years ago. She hadn't wanted to hurt Gwen's feelings by tossing them, but Karen felt her mother had done her duty by those slippers long ago.

"Come in," Karen said uncomfortably. As she wiggled up in bed, she thought how odd it was to see her mother up at this hour. The night was Karen's time.

Mrs. Lewis pulled over the chair from Karen's desk. "I'm just not tired," she explained.

"Mom, you're usually yawning before the dishes are done."

"I don't know, I've got a lot on my mind, I suppose."

Karen waited. Her mother wasn't one to discuss her own problems. Whatever was on her mind was spelled K-A-R-E-N.

"Were you serious about going to see your grandmother?"

This wasn't what Karen had expected. Her mother had seemed totally cool with the idea of her going to visit Vivian. At dinner, she had even said it was important to stay close to her father's family. "I thought you wanted me to visit."

Mrs. Lewis, who was never at a loss for words, fumbled around a little before she said, "Well, yes, I do. But your grandmother isn't the easiest person in the world to get along with." She smiled crookedly. "Take it from me. I bumped heads with Vivian many a time."

"It's only going to be a weekend in New York, Mom. I don't think she's going to give me a hard time."

"No."

Karen looked at her mother curiously. "What's really bothering you?"

"I'm not sure. Perhaps I'm worried visiting Vivian will bring up unpleasant memories for you."

Karen fiddled with her blanket. They were treading on dangerous ground. She and her mother never talked much about her father's death. She wondered how much she had confided in her mom at the time.

"Mom," Karen said, "those memories are a part of my life. There's nothing wrong with having them back. Besides, there are things I'd like to know about Dad that only Vivian can tell me."

"That's true," Mrs. Lewis admitted.

"And let's face it," Karen said, lightening her voice, "I wouldn't mind a trip into the city, staying in an apartment overlooking Central Park."

Her mother smiled a little. "Good reasons, all."

Feeling like the practical one for a change, Karen added, "Besides, by the time I call Vivian to make the arrangements, she could have moved back to London. Or forgotten who I am."

Mrs. Lewis looked aghast at the thought.

"Joke, Mom."

Mrs. Lewis sighed. "Sorry. I just worry about you."

If you only knew the half of it, Karen thought to herself. But all she said was, "I can take care of myself."

Her mother didn't say anything, but Karen could clearly read her look as *Yeah, right.*

Mrs. Lewis got up. "I guess I'll get back in bed and read for a while." With a bit of embarrassment, she asked, "Would you like me to tuck you in?"

"Mom!"

"You used to like it when you were a little girl."

Karen softened. "Okay, if you want to."

Her mother came over, smoothed down the comforter, and tucked it in around Karen. Then she gave her daughter a kiss on the forehead. "Sweet dreams, honey."

If only, Karen thought. "Good night, Mom."

But maybe her mother's wish for sweet dreams had found a home inside Karen, because that night, the dreams took a new path.

Perhaps it was because of her impending visit to Manhattan, but Karen found herself in the city. She was dreaming with the same brightness and intensity, though, and New York, if that's where she was, was all smooth steel and glass. Maybe it wasn't Manhattan, though, because everything was clean, and the sidewalks, with the sun shining down on them, held the same tiny diamonds that the river had.

As she walked along, sometimes passing people, sometimes alone, Karen could feel a sense of expectation building inside of her. It felt big, like climbing up a roller coaster, but without the release of the slide down. Aimlessly, she wandered around, with the feeling filling her up until it was more uncomfortable than pleasurable.

Then suddenly she knew what she was waiting for. She turned around, and there was Mark, looking so glad to see her that she wanted to cry; somehow he knew she felt exactly the same way.

He reached out to her, and she gave him her hand.

Their fingers entwined, and Karen thought she could feel every single point where their skin met. Looking into her eyes, Mark lifted his other hand and touched her cheek. And then, in one wonderful moment, the roller coaster finally dove down.

CHAPTER 4

Mark turned to feel the pellets of hot water beating against his face and eyes, but even that wasn't enough to wake him up. He still felt caught in his dreams, though he couldn't exactly remember them. That girl, Karen, she was there, but how or why was a mystery.

Well, he had to get to school. He couldn't stand around washing his brain all day. He toweled off quickly and grabbed his robe. With Rosanna around, he wanted to be careful he had something on at all times.

Of all the housekeepers his father had found for them over the years, Rosanna was probably Mr. Kennedy's most unusual choice. For one thing, she was young and pretty good looking. And where the other housekeepers were so tough and flinty they could have been sergeants in the army, Rosanna was a hippie-dippie type. Mark expected her to start burning incense any day now. He had already found her listening to his father's old Cream records. Oh well, at least Brian liked her, which was more than could be said for most of the hired-help parade.

As he entered the bedroom to get dressed, the first thing Mark noticed was a big lump under his covers. Creeping up quietly, Mark snuck his hands under the bunched blankets, found his target, and began tickling.

"N-o-o!" Brian shrieked in delight.

"The tickle monster finds a delicious morsel in his bed, and you know what he has to do?"

"What?"

"Tickle!" Mark laughed as he lunged again.

Finally, Brian had to come up for air. His cheeks were flushed and his eyes were sparkling, and just seeing his little brother so happy made Mark's heart hurt.

"What is going on in here!" Paul Kennedy stood in the doorway glaring at the boys. "I told you last night, I have the day off. For once, I don't have to get up at the crack to get to the studio, and you two are yowling like dogs. How inconsiderate can a person be?"

You ought to know the answer to that, Mark thought. But he only muttered, "Sorry."

Brian's happy expression faded to the slightly nervous look he usually wore when his father was around. Fortunately, with his father's busy work schedule that wasn't often.

"Sorry," Brian echoed quietly.

"Well, now that I'm up, I guess we should have breakfast together," Mr. Kennedy said unenthusiastically.

Mark shrugged. "I'll get dressed. You too, bud," he told Brian.

As he threw on his shirt and jeans, Mark grumbled to himself about his father, Mr. Big Shot television director. He acted like he was Steven Spielberg, but all he ever directed were soap operas. He couldn't even hold on to one of those jobs for very long; that's why he was always moving them back and forth between coasts.

But by the time Mark sat down in front of Rosanna's slightly soggy waffles, he had gotten himself together. Mark had learned long ago that the best way to deal with his father was to say little and react even less.

Mr. Kennedy's mood had improved. "These look good, Rosanna," he said, as he dug in.

"Thanks," she replied as she plunked a glass of milk down in front of Brian.

"Do I have to drink it?" Brian asked, making a face.

Before Mr. Kennedy could answer, Rosanna said, "Hey, nothing tastes better with waffles than milk."

"She's right, Bri," Mark added, hoping to avoid a scene.

Brian looked at Mark and then Rosanna. "Okay."

Mark stabbed at his own waffle. It was good that Brian

had given in, but a part of Mark hated the way Brian was already learning to back down. Of course, he had learned that tack from his big brother. No one was a better backer-downer than Mark.

"We've got to talk about Thanksgiving," Mr. Kennedy said.

"Why?" Mark asked. "It's two months away."

"Flights fill up early. I want to get you two reservations for California."

"We're going to see Mom?" Brian asked hopefully.

Mr. Kennedy nodded.

"You said flights for us. Aren't you going?" Mark asked. His parents weren't divorced, but sometimes their marriage seemed as much off as on. The status varied like the weather.

"I have to work," Mr. Kennedy said stiffly.

"Over Thanksgiving?"

"On Wednesday and the following Monday."

Mark didn't say anything. He and Brian would be in school those days, too, but if his father didn't want to come to California, that was all right with him.

"Do you want to fly out Wednesday evening or Thursday morning?" Mr. Kennedy asked.

"Wednesday, I guess. It will give us a little more time with Mom."

Rosanna stuck her head out of the kitchen. "Mr. Kennedy, I'll be wanting the holiday off. That's all right, isn't it?"

Mr. Kennedy shrugged. "I suppose. I'll find something to do on Thanksgiving."

For an instant, Mark felt sorry for his father, but just for an instant. It was his father who had insisted on the three of them moving to New York, so now he was here. Let him scramble for a holiday invitation if he had to.

Breakfast moved at a snail's pace, at least it seemed that way. Mr. Kennedy talked a little about what was happening on *Bright Day*, his soap opera. Both of Mark's parents had worked on the soaps since before he was born, so he had grown up hearing about Erica and Marlena and Luke and Laura and all the gossip of that particular world. It didn't interest him in the least. It did, however, come in handy when he was meeting a new crowd, especially the girls. They always seemed to want to know the inside television dope. Mark was definitely tuned out to the breakfast chatter, but then he heard his name.

"Do any of your friends babysit, Mark?"

A vision of Jenny Cullen trailed by a couple of toddlers flashed into his mind. It faded quickly. "I don't know."

"Well, could you ask around? I may need someone for Saturday nights."

Mark knew better than to inquire about his father's plans.

"I'd ask you," Mr. Kennedy continued, "but it seems like you've already got an active social life going."

Mark shrugged. Yeah, he hung around with the kids, but mostly they just moved from house to house, goofing off. He wasn't sure he wouldn't rather spend the evening with Brian.

Then suddenly it was time to get to school, and instead of having too much time, they were running late.

"Do you want me to drive you?" Mr. Kennedy asked, clearly hoping the answer would be no.

"I'll go," Rosanna said cheerfully.

"Do you mind dropping me off, too?" Mark asked. She always drove Brian, but him only sometimes. He could have made the bus if he hurried, but he didn't want to wait at the bus stop this morning.

"Course not." Rosanna helped Brian on with his jacket.

As they drove along, Mark glanced sideways at Brian. It had been such a surprise when he was born, almost six years ago. Mark had been going on ten, and they were living in California at the time. No one had really told him about a baby coming, and the thing that Mark remembered most about that time was worrying because his mother was getting so fat. He was already very conscious of the fact that people on television needed to look good. When he had finally told his mother his concerns, she had just laughed at him, which hurt his feelings. But then she explained about the baby and what fun it was going to be for Mark to have a little brother or sister. Mark had been doubtful, and nothing about Brian as a baby had changed his mind. But as his brother had gotten older, he had become more fun, and more Mark's responsibility as well. His parents worked long, often odd hours, and despite the nannies and babysitters, there was a gap that Mark filled. When his father had found a job and moved the boys to Manhattan while Mrs. Kennedy was off making a TV movie in Bali, Mark and Brian had grown even closer. Sometimes Mark felt like he was Brian's real dad.

"Hey, whaddya looking at me like that for?" Brian asked.

"I can't look at you all of a sudden?"

Brian crossed his eyes and gave Mark a goofy smile.

Rosanna glanced away from the road and said, "Your face is going to freeze like that."

Brian clapped his hands and made his smile even sillier.

Ignoring Brian, Rosanna said, "You didn't sound too excited about Thanksgiving, Mark."

Mark shrugged. "It'll be good to see Mom."

"Would you rather be living in L.A.?" Rosanna asked.

"I would," Brian said, his expression more serious now. "It's sunnier there," he noted, looking out the window at the gloomy sky.

"Yeah," Mark agreed, but he wasn't thinking about the weather. As involved in her career as his mother might be, she was a pretty happy-go-lucky character. Why he and Brian hadn't stayed with her, Mark never understood.

"You're lucky," Rosanna said with a little sigh. "All that glamor."

"Do you see much glamor around our house?" Mark scoffed.

"Well, no," Rosanna said uncertainly. "But in L.A. you must have seen a lot of big stars."

"I saw Mickey Mouse at Disneyland," Brian informed her.

"If you watch the soaps, I guess," Mark replied.

"Course I do," Rosanna said. "*All My Children,* then *One Life to Live,* then *General Hospital.* And *Bright Day,* of course."

Mark wondered when she did the housework.

"There's Jamie!" Brian said, as Rosanna pulled up to the school. He wiggled out of his seat belt and was in such a hurry to leave he almost forgot his lunch.

"Can I drive now?" Mark asked. All that school switching had pushed him back a year. Even though he was a sophomore, he was almost sixteen, and had had his learner's permit for what seemed like forever. His dad rarely took him out driving though, so Mark had to make do with crumbs from Rosanna or some of the kids at school. Rosanna was pretty easy, though. Anything that made less work for her.

"Sure," she said, already getting out of the car to change places with him.

Mark loved driving. There was nothing like the feeling of being the one in charge, instead of the person who was just along for the ride. For the mile to his own school, he even pretended that Rosanna was his date. Not that he actually wanted *her* for a date, but the presence of a not-unattractive young woman by his side as he sped down the street stimulated his imagination. Of course, he had to block out her prattling. It seemed to be about *Bright Day* and the girl who played the rich ingenue.

"She's got a Brooklyn accent, totally lame."

"Mmm."

"She must've known somebody to get that job, dontcha think?"

"Mmm-hmm."

"I wish she'd die."

That caught Mark's attention.

"On the show, I mean," Rosanna said.

"Oh." Mark expertly pulled in along the curb. "Well, thanks for letting me drive."

"No problem," Rosanna said, but Mark was already aware of Jenny Cullen talking to a couple of her friends on the school steps. When he joined the group, Jenny said, "Who's the girl in the Beemer?"

Mark was flattered, even if Jenny wasn't the most subtle person in the world. He wasn't about to say "she's our nanny," however, so he just gave Jenny a big smile and a shrug.

Jenny turned away from the other girls and spoke quietly to him. "I didn't know you're the kind of boy that keeps secrets."

"Makes me more interesting, don't you think?"

Jenny's smile was frank. "You're pretty interesting already."

"Then that makes two of us." This kind of banter was so easy for him. He could do it without thinking.

Jenny started to walk toward the school entrance without even a backward glance at her friends, and of course, Mark followed her.

"I'm having a party a week from Saturday. Want to come?"

Mark made his shrug casual. "I guess."

"It's kind of a date thing."

"So I'll get a date."

Jenny glanced over at him as if trying to gauge whether he was joking or not. Finally, she put on her famous Jenny pout, the one designed to put fear into the hearts of both boys and girls.

"The hostess doesn't have a date . . . yet."

Mark had figured that's what she was angling for, but he didn't want to seem too anxious. Oh well, no sense letting her squirm. "You have one now."

Jenny's pout turned into a smile. "Terrific. I don't have all the plans down yet, but I'll keep you posted."

Mark felt obligated to walk Jenny to her locker, even though it was halfway across the school from his. On his way to his first class, he caught sight of Karen. She was standing at the top of the staircase in front of a long window. The sun was shining all around her, as though she was in a halo.

Suddenly Mark's dream came back to him. They had been walking in a city together, maybe New York City.

He had held her hand and touched her cheek. A wave of longing like he had never felt swept over him. As quickly as the feeling had come, it passed, gone and impossible to catch hold of.

"Hey, get out of the way!" A boy bumped him as he hurried past.

Mark realized he was just standing in the middle of the bustling hallway. Embarrassed, he started walking to his class, trying to figure out what it all meant.

Try as he might, he couldn't remember any more of the dream, and by the end of the day, he could barely remember the feeling that had been so overwhelming in the hall. Still, as he slid into his seat in Mrs. Aikman's Shakespeare class, he nervously watched the door, waiting for Karen to come in.

She arrived just as the bell rang, and she didn't look in his direction. Now that he had a chance to observe her without a gauzy glow, she was pretty ordinary. Under normal circumstances, she certainly wouldn't turn any heads. Still, there was something about her. He watched her smile as she borrowed a pencil from the boy across the row from her. The smile was both sweet and sad.

Mrs. Aikman stopped fiddling with her papers and looked up at the class. "As some of you know, I think the best way to read Shakespeare is to read it out loud. Even without knowing every word, you can catch the meaning, especially if someone very good is reading."

Some of the kids laughed. It seemed unlikely that

there were any budding Shakespearian thespians in the group.

Mrs. Aikman acknowledged their doubts with a nod. "All right, we may not capture the melody of Shakespeare immediately, but we've done some reading aloud here and there, and I think it would be fun if we did a bit more assigning parts."

Mark waited for the inevitable. Even if *Bright Day* wasn't *Macbeth,* his mother was a pretty good actress, and some of her ability had rubbed off on him. Mrs. Aikman knew it, too. He had been one of the kids who had done some reading aloud. Sure enough, she pretended to look around the class, but what she said was, "Mark, would you mind being our Romeo?"

Mark gave a noncommittal, "No problem."

What he hadn't expected was Mrs. Aikman's choice for his Juliet. Even though Karen was in the forefront of his brain, he figured Mrs. Aikman had her eye on one of the showier girls for the role.

But no, without hesitation, she asked Karen to read that role.

Mark was relieved they could do their reading sitting down. He wasn't feeling all that steady. What was this all about anyway? Dreams, weird feelings, and now Mrs. Aikman throwing them together like some demented casting agent.

Mrs. Aikman picked out a scene, which thankfully wasn't the famous balcony scene with its sweet, even sugary passages. Still, there weren't too many places to go in the play where romance wasn't the focus. Mrs. Aik-man told them they could begin with:

> "Ah, Juliet, if the measure of thy joy
> Be heaped like mine . . ."

Mark began, trying to ignore the other students rustling their pages, looking for the right passage, as well as Karen, who was fidgeting across from him.

When it was her turn, Karen cleared her throat and, as Juliet, picked up where he left off, ending with:

> "But my true love is grown to such excess
> I cannot sum up sum of half my wealth."

Mrs. Aikman interrupted them. "Mark, nicely read, but can you tell me what Romeo's saying?"

Mark looked down at the page. It really hadn't made too much sense. "I guess he's glad to see her."

"That's right, and he wonders whether she is as glad to see him. Is she, Karen?"

Karen didn't need to study the passage. She just nodded and said, "She thinks she's in love."

CHAPTER 5

Karen jumped out of bed, thinking she had overslept and was late for school. Then she remembered it was Saturday.

Before she woke up, she'd been dreaming that Mimi was giving her a perm. When she'd looked in the mirror her hair was in a curly upsweep that made her look like the Bride of Frankenstein. As Karen made her way to the bathroom it hit her that this was the day Mimi was going to do her makeover. Karen wondered glumly if this was one of those dreams that was going to come true.

About a half hour later, Gwen flew into Karen's room without bothering to knock. "When's she coming?"

Karen dropped her brush down on the dresser and turned away from the mirror. "I should never have told you."

"Did you tell your mother?" Gwen asked slyly.

"She and Don left early to go to that flea market."

"That's not an answer," Gwen promptly replied.

"There was nothing to tell."

"Right. Mimi's going to do a complete makeover on you, and you think Barbara's not going to notice? My dad, maybe not, Barbara, no way."

Karen glanced back at the mirror. "Mimi's not a magician, you know. Even if she was, I'm not going to let her do anything drastic . . ." *like give me a perm,* Karen added silently. "She'll probably throw some lipstick on me and call it a makeover." Maybe she could dampen Gwen's interest in this event.

Gwen made a face. "You need more than that. Mimi always looks awesome; she may be able to do something with you."

Well, that was depressing, Karen thought. *Put down by a twelve-year-old.* Gwen assumed she hadn't mentioned the makeover because Barbara would tell Karen to forget it. Her mother might not like it, but she'd never just put her foot down and say no. The real reason Karen hadn't said anything was that she had just as many doubts about the results as Gwen.

"How about some breakfast?" Gwen asked, her thoughts already shifting away from Karen's new look to food.

"I'm not hungry," Karen said. "Go make yourself cereal or something."

"I thought it might be fun to make pancakes together. Like we used to do in the old days? With those cute raisin eyes?"

Karen laughed at Gwen's plaintive tone. "You little fraud. You don't care a thing about doing something together. You just want pancakes, and you know I make them better than you do."

Gwen looked caught. Then she laughed. "Okay, I admit it. I'm dying for your pancakes."

Throwing her arm around Gwen's shoulder, Karen said, "I can't resist honesty. Pancakes it is."

Making breakfast together turned out to be fun. Karen managed to keep the subject away from her so-called makeover, engaging Gwen in conversation about the latest books she was reading. By the time breakfast was ready, Karen had almost forgotten what was in store for her.

Just as they were sitting down to eat, the phone rang.

"You get it," Gwen said, eyeing the steaming pancakes.

"It's probably for you. Unless it's Mimi telling me she can't make it," Karen replied, brightening a little at the thought. Mimi had had to cancel last Saturday for a babysitting job. Maybe Karen would luck out again.

But by now, Gwen was sitting down, picking out the little raisin eyes of her pancake, and the phone was on the third ring.

"Oh, all right." Karen hurried to grab the phone. She had barely said hello, when a voice she didn't recognize said, "Karen?"

"Yes."

"This is Vivian."

For a split second, the name didn't register. Then Karen said, "Oh, hello, uh, Vivian." If she didn't want to be called Grandmother, Karen wasn't going to push it.

"How are you, my dear?"

"Fine. I'm sorry I haven't answered your letter yet . . ."

"So you did receive it."

Karen felt like a fool, or worse, like a little kid. "Yes, but you see—"

"As it turns out," Vivian interrupted, "I don't know how long I'm going to be in the city after all, and I did want to see you before I had to leave again."

"I'd like to see you, too."

"Have you talked to your mother about coming to visit?"

"Sure. I mean, she said it would be fine."

There was an uncomfortable pause.

"When would be good for you?" Karen finally asked.

"I know I shall be here for at least another month. Any weekend would do."

Karen's calendar was totally empty of course, but some stubborn part of her didn't want Vivian to think she could disappear for years and then expect Karen to come at the snap of her fingers. She supposed that was why she hadn't responded to the letter right away—that and a case of the jitters about meeting Vivian after all this time. "I have a couple of things coming up. Why don't I talk to Mom and get back to you?"

Vivian sound disappointed, Karen was happy to note. "I understand, of course. I know how busy young girls are today. Take down my phone number and call me as soon as you're ready to make plans."

Feeling like a fraud, Karen jotted down the number and promised her grandmother that she'd call soon.

As she hung up, another dream she'd had last night, before the silly hairdo one, came washing over. Maybe it was because Vivian had reappeared in her life, but it was the second dream she had had in recent days about her father. In the first one, she had just seen him, standing in front of her house. Eagerly, she had run toward him, but he disappeared. Last night, he was walking away from a young Karen, who was crying and saying over and over, "I'm sorry."

She had been awakened by the shriek of tires and a loud, terrifying crash. Somehow, she had forgotten all about the dream until this moment. She took a second or two to compose herself before she turned back to Gwen. She didn't want her sister to see how upset she was.

Gwen had made considerable headway into her pancakes by the time Karen came back to the breakfast table. Karen wasn't very hungry now.

"Was that your grandmother?" Gwen asked, not bothering to wipe the thread of butter that was making its way down her chin.

"Yes, Vivian."

"Is she calling about that trip to New York?"

Karen nodded.

"You have all the luck," Gwen said enviously. "I guess your grandmother's loaded. At least that's what my dad says."

Karen shrugged and picked up her fork. A lot of good it did her. She wondered how long it had been since she'd even received a Christmas present from her grandmother.

"So when are you going?" Gwen asked, not noticing Karen's change in mood.

"I haven't decided yet. Maybe I won't go at all."

"But you practically said you would."

Again Karen shrugged. Now there were two things she didn't want to think about, New York and the makeover; but any hopes of forgetting the latter were dashed when Mimi pounded at the back door as the girls were clearing the table.

"Oh, you're here," Karen said unenthusiastically.

Mimi didn't take it personally. "Now, don't be worried, Karen, I've told you a million times, this is going to be fun."

"Will you do me, too?" Gwen asked hopefully as she rinsed a milk glass.

Before Mimi could answer, Karen said, "I don't think so."

"Why not?" Gwen pouted.

"Well, for one thing, you don't have Mom or Don's permission."

"You don't either."

"I'm old enough to make this decision for myself."

Mimi was on Gwen's side. "Come on, don't be such a stick. What harm can a little makeup do? I won't even cut her hair."

Startled, Karen said, "Are you going to cut my hair?"

"We'll see," Mimi replied in a soothing voice. Turning to Gwen she said, "Let's see how it goes with Karen. Maybe I can do a little something for you."

Satisfied, Gwen left the kitchen. Karen, on the other hand was anything but satisfied. "You know, we've never talked about just what you had in mind, Mimi."

Mimi laughed and picked up a leftover pancake from the platter and nibbled on it. "Let's just play it by ear, okay?"

Without even giving Karen time to clean up the kitchen, Mimi led her upstairs into the spacious, old-fashioned bathroom she shared with Gwen. She flopped down the cover of the toilet seat and pointed at Karen to sit.

Out of the enormous backpack she was carrying, Mimi pulled scissors and a box of henna.

"What's that?" Karen pointed suspiciously to the box.

"You do have some red highlights in your hair, Karen. The henna will bring them out."

"You can't dye my hair," Karen said nervously.

"It's not dye. It's natural stuff. Henna. The Egyptians were using it to color their hair when they were building the pyramids."

When Karen had been eight she had had her tonsils out. She remembered trying desperately to get off the table before being wheeled into the operating room. The same impulse struck her now.

But as she tried to get up, Mimi's hand gently pushed her back down. "Karen, you want to look different, I know you do."

It was true. She looked different in her dreams, she knew that. More alive somehow. Maybe there was a way to bring that transformation into reality. She felt herself giving up. "All right," she said, with resignation. "Just do it."

For the next couple of hours, Karen tried not to think about what was happening. She certainly didn't look in the mirror. Rinses in, rinses out, and then the reappearance of the scissors. Karen didn't even bother to argue. Mimi seemed to have an infinite number of things to talk about as she worked, everything from her mom's midlife crisis to gossip about one of their history teachers dating a mechanic from Ed's Garage.

"Oh, speaking of dating," Mimi said as she snipped away at Karen's hair, "I guess I better tell you about Mark and Jenny."

Karen's stomach took a belly flop. "What about them?"

"Jenny Cullen is having some kind of big party tonight, and Mark's her date."

"So?" Karen said, trying to sound nonchalant.

"Don't even bother pretending you're not interested, because I don't believe you."

Suddenly, Mimi seemed all too bossy. "Fine. Don't believe me," Karen snapped.

But Mimi, as usual, was unflappable. "See what I mean? If you really didn't care, you wouldn't be upset. But don't worry. Mark Kennedy is going to sit up and take notice once I'm done with you."

Without any encouragement from Karen, Mimi went on to describe how Jenny's parties were usually beer bashes, conveniently planned when her parents weren't home.

"How do you know?" Karen finally asked.

"Because for about one second, I was in with Jenny's crowd."

"You never told me that!"

"I'm not exactly proud of it." Mimi grimaced. "I don't know what got into Jenny, but she decided that the preppie world needed a token free spirit, so she asked me to one of her parties."

"And you went?"

"Yes." Mimi put down her scissors. "I went. I was curious, and okay, I thought it might be interesting to run with the fun crowd."

"So what happened?"

"People drank a lot of beer, then some of them threw

up. The ones that managed to contain the heaves were making out. Frankly, between vomiting and making out, I would have chosen vomiting. Instead, I left. Nobody noticed."

"That does sound like fun," Karen said. "Well, if that's what Mark is into, for sure I'm not interested." *Could he really be like that?* she wondered. Lately he had been so sweet in her dreams.

Karen, snap out of it, she told herself. *You don't know a thing about him. Not when the sun is shining.*

Without bidding, a recent dream came back to her. Mark was telling her about his little brother. Such love lit his face when he spoke about the boy that Karen had felt her eyes fill with tears. In fact, the same thing was happening right now.

"Did some hair get in your eyes?" Mimi asked

"I . . . I think so."

"Just brush it out."

"Mimi, I'm getting tired of sitting here."

"But I've got to dry your hair, then put on your makeup. Beauty hurts, you know."

"Tell me about it. Well, just let me get up and stretch."

Reluctantly, Mimi stepped back and let Karen get up.

"Now don't look yet."

"No problem."

"You're going to be adorable," Mimi assured her. "Mark's going to forget he even knows Jenny Cullen's name."

"Mimi . . ." Oh, what was the use? Karen flopped back

down on the toilet lid. "Do you promise? He's really going to know I'm alive?"

Mimi clapped her hands, almost stabbing herself with the scissors. "Finally, finally, you admit you like him. All you ever said before was that you dreamed about him."

"You wore me down," Karen muttered.

Mimi began clipping again with renewed vigor. "You know, I never really felt like your best friend before. Now, I do."

"Of course you're my best friend," Karen said shyly. But Mimi was right. It was Mimi who had done all the confiding in their relationship, talking about her parents' divorce and the boy she had met during her August vacation in Maine. Karen had liked hearing all this stuff, so normal, but most of the conversation had been one way. Mimi had once said she liked Karen because she was such a good listener, and Karen had almost laughed out loud. Now it felt good to be confiding in Mimi, but a little scary, too.

"You know, if you like him, you're going to have to talk to him, too," Mimi said, blowing Karen's hair dry. "Just looking gorgeous won't be enough."

Best friends or not, Karen wasn't ready yet to tell Mimi that she did more than talk to Mark—it just happened to be at night when they both were sleeping. "I do talk to him in English class—a little."

"Well, that's good," Mimi said encouragingly. "That's a start."

"But Mimi, if he's really dating Jenny . . ."

"He'll drop her. She's not that interesting."

"Maybe he doesn't want interesting."

Before Mimi could counter that observation, Gwen came into the bathroom. Karen tried to gauge her expression. It seemed like surprise.

"Wow. I mean, you sure look different."

"Now, don't say another word," Mimi frowned. "Not until I'm done."

The hair drying continued. Then the makeup began. "Look up," Mimi kept insisting, until Karen was sure she knew every crack in the ceiling. Still, the makeup didn't take very long. At least, not compared to everything that had gone before.

Gwen sat cross-legged on the cold bathroom floor, watching. "You're going to do me next, right?"

She couldn't look that bad, Karen figured, if Gwen still wanted Mimi to have a go at her.

Finally, finally, Mimi was finished. She marched Karen over to the bathroom mirror and stood behind her as they both gazed into the mirror.

Now Karen knew why Gwen had looked so surprised. She looked utterly changed. Her hair had a definite reddish cast, and where it once had just sort of hung around her shoulders, it now curled under in a flattering pageboy that barely grazed her jaw. Whatever Mimi had done with her eyes, they now looked twice their usual size, and while they weren't Mimi's incredible summer sky color, they were deep, midnight blue, suddenly sensuous. Karen rarely wore lipstick, but now her lips were colored with a raspberry shade that brought her whole face to life.

"Say something," Mimi demanded.

"I don't know what to say."

"You like it, don't you?"

"Oh, you've got to like it Karen," said Gwen, who was trying to look in the mirror, too. "This is better than the makeovers they had on *Oprah* last week."

"I feel different," Karen finally said. Could how you looked really affect the way you felt?

"Well, I think you look beautiful," Mimi declared. "Beea-u-t-i-ful!"

Gwen interrupted. "I think somebody's knocking at the door."

"Will you get it?" Karen asked. "I'm not sure I want to see anybody right now."

"Well, I don't know why," Mimi complained. "You look better than you ever did."

"Get it Gwen, please."

"Okay, okay, but then it's my turn, right, Mimi?"

"Sure."

As Gwen left the room, Karen turned to Mimi. "How am I ever going to do this when you're not around? I don't know how to get my hair like this. And I'm no good at putting on makeup."

"Don't worry, I'll teach you. It's not that big a deal."

Karen looked back at her reflection. "This is so weird. In a good kind of way, I mean."

Gwen lumbered back into the bathroom. "There's

some guy downstairs. Mark. He wants to see you, Karen."

"Mark Kennedy?" Karen asked, shocked.

"He just said Mark."

"Go down, and tell Mark she'll be right there," Mimi instructed.

"Now?" Karen squeaked.

"Of course, now." Mimi shook her head. "Boy, am I good or what? I told you I'd get you Mark, but even I didn't think I could do it this fast!"

CHAPTER 6

Later, when she thought back on it, Karen was surprised that seeing Mark in her house lacked the magnetic feelings of her dreams. As she walked down the stairs to the hallway, she was aware only of the nervous twitching in her stomach and the odd sensation of having her hair swing around her chin.

"Hello, Mark." She searched his face for a reaction to her new look. She didn't see admiration. Just an odd, quizzical look.

"Hi." *She looks different,* he thought. *More glamorous. Not like my Karen.* Then he wondered where the word *my* had come from.

They stood there contemplating each other for a few

minutes. A rush of thoughts flew through Karen's mind. Had his date with Jenny fallen through? Or maybe he wanted to take her to the party instead. Why didn't he say something?

"Uh, Karen, it's about tonight."

Karen's heart leaped up.

"My dad's going out tonight, and he asked me to find a babysitter for my little brother, Brian."

When Karen just stared at him, he felt it necessary to keep talking. "He's really a great kid. I would babysit him myself, but I have plans for tonight."

Well, goody for you, Karen thought angrily.

"I know it's awfully short notice," Mark stumbled along, "but I wouldn't want Brian to stay with just any-one. . . ." his words sort of died out.

"I don't think I can," Karen finally replied stiffly.

"Oh. Yeah, it's kind of late," he said. His father had told him on Monday he needed a babysitter for tonight, and Karen had come to mind right away. He knew he should have asked her earlier, but it had never seemed the right time. He had even told his father he couldn't find anyone, but neither could his dad, and he'd insisted Mark keep trying.

Karen was ready to turn around, go back upstairs, and just leave him standing there, when suddenly she heard a voice say, *Go!* She looked around, half expecting to see someone else in the hallway, but there were just the two of them.

Obviously Mark hadn't heard anything. He continued

to stand there, looking embarrassed. "Well, maybe some other time. You do babysit, don't you?"

Karen, regaining a little of her composure, said, "Sometimes." Then the voice said again, more quietly this time, *Go*.

"I'd better be leaving," Mark said uncomfortably, wondering why Karen was suddenly looking so odd.

"I . . . I might be able to do it." Voices notwithstanding, she wasn't ready to just cave in.

"Really?" Mark brightened. "That would be great."

"Give me your phone number. I'll call you in a half hour or so and let you know for sure." She found a piece of paper and a pencil on the hall table and handed it to him.

Mark scribbled his phone number. "Just let me know as soon as you can."

The impelling force of the voice was gone, and Karen wasn't happy that she had conceded even this much to Mark. "I'll call," she said curtly.

Mark knew when he was being dismissed. "Uh, thanks. By the way, you look good." It seemed a little limp, even to his own ears, but he felt like he owed Karen something.

She just nodded and opened the door for him. When he was gone, she leaned against the door for a moment. What was going on here? Was she really supposed to go and babysit stupid Mark's stupid brother? And if so why? None of this was making any sense.

Slowly, she made her way back upstairs. Mimi and Gwen were still in the bathroom. Now Gwen was getting the makeover. Karen hoped it would be more effective for Gwen than it had been for her.

"So?" Mimi demanded, as Karen appeared in the doorway. She put down the pale peach lipstick she was using on Gwen. "Spill!"

"He had my evening all planned for me."

"Really?" Mimi squealed.

"Oh yeah. He wanted me to babysit for his brother."

"That was it?" Gwen's newly made-up face wore a disappointed expression.

"That was it." Karen studied Gwen. The makeup was subtle, but more than a twelve-year-old should be wearing. Her mother wasn't going to approve.

"Well, I hope you told him you couldn't do it," Mimi said indignantly.

Karen didn't want to say that that had been her first inclination, but a mysterious voice had urged her otherwise. "I could use the money," she said evasively.

"But you don't want him to think of you as a babysitter," Gwen told her.

Love counseling from a kid. How low could she sink?

"On the other hand," Mimi said thoughtfully, "it would get you in the door."

"Yeah, in the door of his house. But he's not going to be home."

"So are you going to do it?" Mimi asked.

Karen had known the answer to that as soon as the word *Go* had reverberated through her brain. "I suppose I am."

"So we'll look at this as a start. Didn't he say anything about how you looked?"

"He said I looked good."

Mimi broke into a smile. "Well, there you are."

"I don't think he meant it."

"Karen! Why do you always have to be such a pessimist?"

Mimi's question stuck with Karen the rest of the day. It was there in the back of her mind through the slightly heated exchange she had with her mother and Don, who couldn't understand how they could leave two daughters at home one way and come home to them looking quite different. It hung with her as she dutifully called Mark and told him she would sit, yes, seven would be fine. And now it was still playing around the edges of her mind as she got dressed for an evening with the wrong Kennedy brother. The young one.

Well, why shouldn't she be a pessimist? Hadn't she learned not to trust a world where one day you could be a perfectly normal child like everyone else and the next find out that your father had died in a car accident, and now you were going to be different from your friends, the girl without a father.

But you really weren't exactly normal before, a secret part of herself asserted. *And still aren't.*

"I don't want to think about that," she said aloud.

"About what?" Mrs. Lewis had slipped into the room without Karen noticing.

"Nothing," Karen replied defensively.

Mrs. Lewis let it pass. "Karen, I don't think I told you this afternoon how pretty you look."

"You really like it?"

Her mother reached out and touched Karen's hair. "It was just such a surprise."

"I felt like I needed a change."

"You know, the shorter cut looks great." She touched Karen's hair.

Karen almost smiled. "But the color . . ."

"It's a little, uh, red, for my taste, but . . ."

"It'll wash out, Mom, don't worry."

"And the makeup, maybe a little softer. Of course, on Gwen . . ."

Now Karen did smile. "Yeah, it was way too much for Gwen, but you know Mom, I think it made her feel pretty, too. That counts for something."

Mrs. Lewis nodded slowly. "You're right. I should have thought about that."

Karen pulled a ratty old flannel shirt out of her closet. She had given Mark her best shot this afternoon. No way was she going to get dressed up just on the off chance he hadn't already left for Jenny's when she arrived.

"So, this is a new sitting job for you?" her mother asked conversationally.

Karen nodded. "The brother of a kid I know from school." That sounded casual enough.

"And it's just a couple of blocks away?"

"One of those big houses down by the ravine."

"I've always wanted to go inside those houses. I bet it's gorgeous."

"I'll give you a full report."

"Leave the phone number," Mrs. Lewis said, as she turned to leave.

"Mom."

Mrs. Lewis stood in the doorway. "What, sweetie?"

"I was thinking about Daddy before you came in."

"But you didn't want to. Isn't that what you said?"

Karen didn't answer.

"There were so many good times with your father. I hope you think about those, Karen."

Karen hesitated. She wasn't sure she wanted to get into all this now, but she felt compelled to ask. "Do you remember those dreams I had? The ones before Daddy died?"

Her mother looked startled. "I thought you didn't remember much about that time. After the accident, I asked you more than once if you recalled any special dreams about your dad, and you acted as if you didn't know what I was talking about."

So there was the answer to one question. Her mother did remember about the dreams. And now that her mother mentioned it, Karen recalled feigning ignorance about the dreams. She had felt so guilty. She hadn't been able to save her father.

"I tried to forget," Karen replied, playing with the truth, "but lately, things have been coming back to me."

"You had dreams that your father was going to die," Mrs. Lewis said carefully.

"But it was more than that."

Before either one of them could say anything else, Gwen bounded into the room. "Aren't we going to the movies, Barbara? We're going to be late."

"In a minute, Gwen," Mrs. Lewis said, distracted.

"Dad's already in the car."

The moment had passed. Karen looked at her watch. "You'd better go. I'm going to be late myself if I don't get a move on."

"Don't worry about this, Karen," her mother said. "It's probably best to forget about it."

Gwen looked at them curiously. "About what? The makeovers?"

"No," was all Karen said as she grabbed her purse. As for her mother's comment, Karen ignored it. It was clear that her mother was uncomfortable with the subject of Karen's dreams, just as she always had been. It was all coming back to Karen now. Even though her mother had tentatively asked questions about the dreams right after the car accident, and even later, Karen had always sensed that she didn't really want to know the answers. Then there had been silence, and even a young Karen knew that it was because her mother was frightened.

It was almost dark as Karen made her way to Mark's. The weather had turned warmer, into Indian summer, and the walk was so pleasant Karen didn't feel the need to hurry. Her house was one of the oldest in the neighborhood, but down by the ravine where Mark lived, the homes were newer and much more impressive. She found Mark's house easily, but she stood outside for a few moments, wondering exactly what she was doing there. Finally, she couldn't put it off any longer. It was already a little past seven. Quickly, leaving herself no out, she rang the bell.

An older version of Mark answered the door. But Mark's father didn't have his son's easy smile. Mr. Kennedy's look was impatient, as if he was aware of every second Karen was late.

"I'm Karen Genovese," she said nervously.

"Well, come in."

The house was lovely, as she had known it would be. The ample entryway led into a large living room whose most distinctive feature was its wraparound windows. Although it was too dark to tell, they must look out on the ravine and the wooded areas that surrounded it.

Mr. Kennedy looked at his watch. "I'm almost ready to leave. Why don't you say hello to Brian while I finish dressing?"

Wasn't there a Mrs. Kennedy? Karen wondered. Then

she recalled that Mark had said his father needed a babysitter. Maybe they were divorced.

"He's in his room. It's this way."

Dutifully, she followed Mr. Kennedy past the gourmet kitchen, down a long hall. He pointed to a closed door. "In there," he said, before disappearing into his own bedroom.

Karen knocked softly. When there was no answer, she opened the door.

A boy with hair like Mark's was on the bed, a whole army of Ninja figures surrounding him. Intent on whatever scenario he was playing with the two figures in his hand, he barely looked up when Karen said hello.

"I'm going to be staying with you tonight. My name is Karen."

Finally, Brian looked up. At first he seemed puzzled. "I know you, don't I?"

"I don't think so," Karen said, but she had to acknowledge that she, too, felt a jolt of familiarity upon seeing his face. "But maybe we've seen each other in the neighborhood," she added, although she didn't believe that was the case. "I just live up the hill."

Brian seemed to lose interest in their mutual recognition. "Do you know how to play Ninja warriors?"

"I've never played before, but I could learn."

"Oh, good," Brian said enthusiastically. He waved her over to the bed.

Karen couldn't help but smile. There was no doubt

this was an endearing child. She joined him on the bed and listened as Brian explained seriously who all the different characters were and their various qualities.

"See, this one, Asura, he's the bravest. He has the smallest sword, but it doesn't matter because he's not afraid of anything. *Anything.*" Brian continued, "The world doesn't have to be afraid because Asura protects the people."

"How do you know all this?" Karen asked, wondering if she was about to hear some metaphysical answer.

"Oh, I watch *Fearless Ninjas* on television. It's a cartoon show."

Karen laughed. Nothing otherworldly there.

"You have a nice laugh."

"Do I?"

"Do you like to sing?"

"I suppose."

"I like to sing. I like to sing at the top of my lungs." With that he broke into a chorus of the Fearless Ninjas' theme song.

Karen looked at Brian, startled. Didn't her father used to say that he liked to sing at the top of his lungs? She was almost sure he did.

Mr. Kennedy interrupted the singing.

"Quiet, Brian. You don't want to break your babysitter's eardrums."

"Oh, it's all right," Karen murmured. It was clear he didn't even remember her name.

"I'm leaving now. I should be home about one or so.

That isn't too late for you." It was more of a statement than a question.

"No, that will be fine." Karen noticed he didn't kiss Brian good night, he just gave them both a quick wave.

When Karen turned back to Brian, the boy's happy mood had dissolved.

"Can I watch television?" he asked, pushing his Ninja warriors aside.

"I suppose so."

Brian led Karen into the family room. The focal point was not the television but an impressive stone fireplace surrounded by photographs. While Brian clicked on the TV, Karen went over to look at them. She expected to see photos of Brian and Mark and perhaps the elusive Mrs. Kennedy, but instead they were all of Mr. Kennedy and various people, some of whom looked vaguely familiar. Finally, it struck her that these were soap opera stars. She watched one or two of the shows in the summer, though she had never really been caught up in them.

"What does your dad do?"

Brian looked at her suspiciously. "What do you mean?"

"What's his job?"

"Oh. He works on a television show. *Bright Days.*"

"He's not an actor, is he?"

"No. He's the director." Brian said it awkwardly, as if he didn't quite know what that meant.

Well that explained a lot, Karen thought. The beautiful house and Mark's air of sophistication. She would have loved to have asked Brian where his mother was, but it might be an upsetting question. Karen knew all too well how awkward it could be when strangers asked about a missing parent.

She sat down next to Brian and tried to keep her mind on the sit com he was watching. Mostly she just watched him.

Karen had to tell herself that she was awake, not in one of her nighttime dreams. That was the way she felt, though, in an altered state, but more alert at her core than she ever thought she could be in the course of the day. What was it about Brian? He was a charmer, but so were several of the kids she had sat for. That wasn't enough to make her want to reach out and wrap her arms around him and hold him as safe and warm and tight as humanly possible.

Not that he would let her do that, as it turned out. Brian may have been a friendly child, but he was also a fairly self-sufficient one. When he got tired, he told Karen he wanted to go to sleep and barely allowed a good-night hug, though he did cling to her hand for a moment before he let her go.

As Karen settled herself in the family room with the Spanish book she had brought, she wondered about the Kennedy boys and their hold on her. Mark and now apparently, Brian. A voice had told her to come here, at least she thought it had, but for what purpose? Certainly not to watch TV and study Spanish during commercials.

Karen wasn't usually the nosy type. She hardly ever

looked at people's stuff in the other houses where she babysat. But with a long evening stretching in front of her and all her senses heightened at being in Mark's house, and with nothing to do but watch the dull Saturday night TV schedule, or worse yet, study, well, a wander through the house was inevitable.

Tossing her Spanish book aside, Karen wandered to the back of the house. Slightly nervous and a little ashamed, she peeked into Mr. Kennedy's room. It was very neat. The dresser surfaces were clear and no clothes were strewn around. Closing the door, she walked past Brian's room to Mark's bedroom, where she had been headed all along.

She didn't quite know what to expect when she opened the door. She hoped there wouldn't be pictures of half-dressed women taped to the wall.

There weren't. Like his father's room, Mark's bedroom was tidy. The only pictures on the wall were a couple of framed shots of a young Mark holding a surfboard, an autographed picture of the rock group Aerosmith and one of Mark, Brian, and a pretty woman who was obviously Mrs. Kennedy.

Karen studied that one. They certainly seemed to adore each other. They were all smiling at each other in the photo, and Mrs. Kennedy was holding the boys tight. She wondered if Mr. Kennedy had been behind the camera, then she thought, probably not. The picture had a professional quality to it.

You really should get out of here, Karen told herself. As interesting as this was, snooping in Mark's room was a little creepy. Walking to the door, Karen noticed a stack of books on Mark's bedstand. *Well,* she reasoned, *one look at his reading material really wouldn't hurt anything.*

There was a stack of four books on the stand. One was his Shakespeare book. Nothing exciting there. There was also a mystery and a crossword puzzle paperback. But it was the book on top that made Karen catch her breath. A book about dreams?

Karen picked it up. It wasn't the same book that Mimi had given her, and as Karen flipped through the pages, she could see that the tone was more flip than her book. Still, why was Mark interested in dream interpretation? Was he having odd dreams, too, or was it just a weird coincidence?

Confused, Karen put the book down where she had found it and hurried back to the television room. She wondered if she should ask Mark about it, but then realized if she did, he would know she had been poking around his room. Maybe there was a way to bring it up in casual conversation, but what would she say? *How did you sleep last night?*

The TV was still on, and Karen left it on, but she picked up her Spanish book once more. Trying to find a comfortable spot on the couch, she finally gave in and just curled up, her head against the armrest and the book propped up in front of her. This, as it turned out, was not the most efficient way to study Spanish. In no time at all she was nodding off. Suddenly there was a door slamming and her name was being called. Clumsily she tried to sit up, as she sputtered to the figure looming over her, "What are you doing here?"

CHAPTER 7

Much later that night, as Mark wearily dragged himself to bed, he wondered how everything could have gone so wrong. When he came home and saw Karen asleep on the couch, his first thought had been how sweet she looked. She reminded him a little of Brian asleep, only without a thumb in the mouth.

He had tried not to scare her. There was nothing worse than waking up and feeling disoriented and vulnerable. But there wasn't much he could think of to do other than softly call out her name.

After her initial embarrassment when she awoke, Karen had seemed glad to see him, especially when he told her he had come home early just because he wanted to. But all the good feeling evaporated when Jenny appeared.

Twisting and turning under the covers, unable to even imagine sleeping, Mark went over the events of the last couple of hours.

He had just been asking Karen if she'd like a Coke or something when he heard the car drive up. He'd never suspected it was Jenny. He thought he had left her behind for the night.

It wasn't that the evening had been so terrible. The party had been all right at first, there was dancing and some making out, and at any other time it might have been fun, but he just couldn't seem to get into it.

Jenny hadn't seemed to notice. She acted like she was having the best time in the world, all giggly and kissy-faced. Her parents were out for the evening and kids felt free to nip from the bottles of beer or liquor that several of them had brought along.

For reasons Mark didn't quite understand, the booze, even the kissing, weren't adding up to much fun. As the night wore on, the effort to look like he was having a good time was proving exhausting. Mark wanted desperately to go home, and finally he had feigned sickness.

"I'm really not feeling well, Jen," he told her. And at that moment he really wasn't.

"What's wrong?"

"I don't know. It's like I'm coming down with something. I've got a headache, and I think I've got a fever."

She placed her delicate hand against his head. "Maybe you do feel a little warm."

It wasn't surprising. With all the kids in Jenny's rec room, it was like a steam bath down there.

"Do you want to go home?"

"I hate to ruin the party." He faked a cough. "I can stick it out, I guess."

"Well, you can't stay if you're sick. I might catch it." She frowned, probably thinking of the kisses they'd exchanged. "I might have already."

Mark just stood there, waiting for her to come to the decision on her own.

"All right," she said with a sigh. "I'll drive you home."

She had tried to be solicitous on the way home, advising him to take a couple of aspirin and go right to bed, but it wasn't really in her nature. By the time she dropped him off, she seemed more than ready to rejoin the party.

But then, for some reason—maybe she had a mustard seed of a conscience after all—she'd come back. The door wasn't locked, and Jenny had walked right in and followed the noise of the television.

"I thought I should . . ." Her eyes darted from Mark to Karen. "What are you doing here?" she asked bluntly.

Karen had let Mark answer. "She's babysitting my little brother."

"And you thought she needed help? You wanted to come home to be with her?"

At that instant, Mark realized that Jenny was right.

Not about helping sit, but that he did want to see Karen. That was why he hadn't been able to enjoy the evening, why he hadn't wanted to kiss Jenny.

But instead of saying so, Mark looked at Jenny, and his feelings turned upside down. All he could see was her anger and then his future at West Ridge disappearing, like water swirling down a drain. That scared him. His feelings for Karen, both in the several dreams he had had about her and in real life, were too strong and too strange. They scared him too. Standing there between both girls, he stuffed his heart in his pocket and followed his head. "I'm sick, Jen. I wasn't thinking about Karen. I forgot she was even here."

Although he tried to avoid looking at her, Mark couldn't help glimpsing Karen's expression out of the corner of her eye. She looked like someone had slapped her across the face. Jenny, on the other hand, wore a satisfied smile.

Karen made the first move. She got up off the couch and announced, "You can take over now, Mark. I'm going home."

Mark had panicked a little. "But how are you going to get there?"

Her laugh was short and harsh. "It's not that far. I'll walk."

Jenny said, "I'll drive you."

"I don't think so," Karen replied curtly, as she gathered her books.

"But it's late," Mark protested.

Karen didn't even bother to answer. She just headed for the door and went out into the darkness of the night.

For Jenny, it was as if Karen didn't exist once she left the house. She had fussed over Mark, insisting on finding him some aspirin, and finally had left when Mark said he felt sick to his stomach.

And now, here tossing in his bed, Mark wondered if a guilty conscience could make you ill. Even though the distance was short, he worried about Karen's midnight walk. He was angry at himself for putting that awful look on Karen's face just because he was scared of Jenny's reaction. And he was afraid to fall asleep because he might have a dream about Karen. The last one had been so joyous and full of light. Now that he had betrayed her, would the dreams turn dark?

He thought about calling Karen's house, hoping that she'd answer, so that he would know she was all right. But what if one of her parents answered? He'd be too chicken to ask for her in the middle of the night, so he still wouldn't know if she was okay. Mark punched his pillow. And what was his dad going to think when he found Mark's note that explained Mark had come home early, and Karen had left?

His dad. He was never the easiest person in the world to get along with, but since they'd moved to West Ridge, he'd been more restless, more grumpy, and he drank more. Brian was nervous around him, and Mark felt he had to protect Brian from their father's moods. Whenever he broached the topic to his mother on the phone, she changed the subject or, when pressed, laughed and said, "Well you know Daddy." Daddy. His father hadn't been Daddy to Mark for a long, long time.

Finally, sleep came.

He was walking with Karen. Mark tried to match his step with hers, but she was always just a little bit ahead. When he finally caught her, she smiled and put her arms around his neck.

Mark drew her closer. There was a soft kiss. Suddenly Karen pulled away and looked at him darkly.

How could her mood change so quickly? Then Mark remembered how he had betrayed Karen. He stiffened, waiting for her to accuse him.

What she said though, was, "What about Brian?"

Brian? For a few seconds, Mark didn't even remember who Brian was, so consumed was he with Karen. Finally, he said, "What about him?"

But all Karen did was sigh and turn away.

The rest of the dream lacked clarity, and though it never turned into the nightmare that Mark had feared, when he finally woke up the next morning, he was sweaty and tired. Maybe he was getting sick after all.

He dragged himself out of bed, though, when he heard a crash. When Mark got out to the kitchen, he was greeted by a big mess. Somehow Brian had managed to knock over not only his orange juice, but his cereal as well. His father, who looked slightly hungover, was wiping and cursing at the same time, while Brian cowered in his chair, too scared to even cry.

"Well, Sleeping Beauty finally awakes," Mr. Kennedy groused at Mark. "Get a towel and help me clean up this mess."

With a quick pat to Brian's head, Mark did as he was told. He worked more efficiently than his father, and in a few minutes, the juice, flakes, and milk were gone.

Mark slid into his chair. "Do you want me to fix you a little more cereal, sport?"

"Forget it," Mr. Kennedy snapped, pouring himself another cup of black coffee. "One breakfast to a customer."

"May I be excused?" Brian asked in a small voice.

Mr. Kennedy dismissed him with a flick of his hand.

"I don't know why Rosanna needs any days off," he muttered. "She just sits around watching the tube when she's here."

Mark didn't bother to answer that. He wasn't hungry at all, but he sipped at his juice.

"So what happened last night? How come that babysitter was gone when I got back?"

"Like I said in the note, I came home early, so Karen left."

"I suppose I have to pay her anyway."

"Dad! She was here for at least three hours. Of course, you do." Then Mark had a great idea. "I could bring the money over to her."

Mr. Kennedy shrugged. He pulled out his wallet and handed over twelve dollars to Mark. "So why did you come home early, anyway?"

"I . . . I wasn't feeling well."

"Are you feeling better now?"

"I guess. What about you?" he ventured.

His father sighed.

"You look kind of sick."

Mr. Kennedy pushed his hand through his hair. "I went to a press party last night for the network. Noisy, loud. Not fun. Besides, all those network honchos are idiots." Mr. Kennedy's voice rose. "They've never even watched a soap, much less know how one runs. But that doesn't stop them having opinions. Lots of damn opinions!"

Uh-oh, Mark thought. He knew where this was going. He had seen it before. Whenever things weren't going well with his father at work, his temper went up a few notches and suddenly everyone was an idiot.

"Sorry," Mark muttered. He then quickly swallowed what was left of his juice and got up. "I guess I'll go give Karen her money."

"Well take Brian with you. I'm going back to bed."

Mark went to get Brian. He would have liked to be alone with Karen, though what he was going to say he wasn't sure. Still, he needed to get Brian out of the line of fire.

Brian was sitting in his room, staring out the window.

"Are you okay?" Mark asked.

"Uh-huh." Brian turned toward Mark. "Why can't we go live with Mom?"

Trust Brian to cut to the chase.

"I don't know, sport. That's just what Mom and Dad have decided."

Brian pursed his lips together. "It's a bad decision. Dangerous."

"Oh, come on, Bri. I know Dad can be a grump, but living here isn't dangerous."

Brian turned back to the window.

"Do you want to come with me?"

"Where are you going?"

"I have to give Karen her money for babysitting you last night."

Brian turned around, looking a little happier. "I liked her."

"Did you?" Mark smiled slightly. "I think she's nice, too."

"You're friends, right?" Brian asked.

"Well, the truth is, Karen might be a little mad at me."

"What did you do?" Brian demanded.

"It's a long story, but I guess I wasn't as nice to her as I could have been."

Brian shook his head and looked like a little old man. "Then we better go over there. I can fix it. She likes me."

Oh, this is normal, Mark thought as they walked over to Karen's. *Now I need Brian to help me with girls.* On the other hand, everyone seemed to fall in love with Brian immediately. Maybe it wasn't such a bad idea for him to come along.

The day turned out to be one of those bright fall ones where the sky is so blue it hurts your eyes. Mark slowed as they came closer to Karen's house. There was a girl in the yard raking leaves, but it wasn't Karen.

Gwen looked up when she saw them approaching. *Uh-oh*, she thought. Karen had been in a terrible mood all morning, and Gwen was pretty sure it had something to do with last night. The little brother looked cute enough. No, it was definitely the big brother who had caused the trouble.

"Hello," she said pleasantly as they came into the yard.

"Is Karen home?" Mark asked.

"She was my babysitter last night," Brian informed her. "Are you her sister?"

"Yes. I'm Gwen. Karen's upstairs. I don't know if she wants to come down."

Mark knew he could just hand over the money to Gwen, but that would blow everything. He stood there until Gwen reluctantly said, "I'll call her."

Gwen took the stairs two at a time. "Hey," she said, crashing into Karen's room. "That Mark guy is downstairs."

Karen didn't even look up from her Shakespeare book. "I'm not here."

"I already told him you were."

Now Karen did glance in Gwen's direction, disgustedly. "Then you have to tell him you were wrong."

"It's not just Mark. It's his little brother, too."

"Brian?" Karen asked, startled. He had been part of the dream last night. She didn't know how she could have had such a romantic dream about Mark when she was so mad at him. Yet there had been something unsettling about the dream as well. Brian was in danger. Karen had felt it in every pore of her body. She had wanted to tell Mark that, but she'd known he wouldn't understand. That figured. Mark was as thick in the dream state as he was in real life.

"So what should I tell them?" Gwen prodded her.

"I guess I'll go down," Karen decided.

Brian was tossing leaves at Mark when Karen stepped into the yard, while Mark, laughing, tried to duck them. When Brian spotted Karen, he ran right to her and brightly said hi. Mark brushed the leaves from his clothes and approached her more trepidatiously.

"Mark said you were mad at him," Brian piped up.

"Did he?" Karen tried to make her tone noncommittal.

"So are you?" Brian persisted.

Mark stepped into the fray. "I need a few minutes alone with Karen. Why don't you help Gwen rake up some leaves."

Gwen looked put out about being lumped together with a kid. Brian, on the other hand, turned to Mark and said, "I was going to help you talk to Karen."

Even Karen couldn't help smiling at that.

"You helped by coming," Mark said. "Now go."

Reluctantly, Brian moved off.

Mark fumbled with the money, pulling it from his pocket. "I thought I should bring this over. From last night."

Coolly, Karen took it. "Thanks." She wasn't going to make this easier by saying anything else.

"Listen, about last night."

"You were pretty clear."

"I did come home because I wanted to see you." There. He had said it.

For some reason, though, this made Karen angry all over again. "Oh, really? Then why did you say the exact opposite to Jenny?"

How could he explain what a coward he had been? He settled for a lame, "I don't know."

"Great answer," Karen said sarcastically. It wasn't like her to be so out there with her emotions, especially with someone she hardly knew. Maybe that was the difference: part of her felt she knew Mark very well, and he'd let her down terribly. She couldn't deny that it felt good to see Mark looking so chastened.

"I guess I owe you an apology."

"I hope that wasn't it."

Karen's curt tone began to grate on Mark. So he had taken the easy way out last night. Did Karen have to rub his nose in it?

"Did Jenny take good care of you?" Karen continued. "After I left, I mean."

"As a matter of fact, she did," Mark replied defiantly.

"Then you made a good choice."

"You know, you're not making any points with me by acting like this." Whenever Mark felt cornered, he turned haughty.

"Oh, I'm not?" Karen couldn't believe the nerve of this guy. He could dish it out, but he sure couldn't take it. "Gee, I guess I'd better try to be a lot nicer. Like Jenny."

"Well, at least she isn't a total—"

Brian came running up to them. "You're fighting," he said accusingly.

Mark calmed down a little. "Yeah, I guess we are."

"Don't do that."

Karen kneeled down next to him. "I'm sorry we're upsetting you, Brian. Mark and I just don't seem to be able to get along."

Brian looked from one to the other. "But why don't you? I thought you really liked each other."

"What made you think that?" Mark asked curiously.

"I had a dream about it."

CHAPTER 8

"Then what happened?" Mimi asked, her eyes wide.

Karen lowered her voice. Even though they were outside, kids were all around them, rushing to get to class. She didn't want anyone to hear.

"It was weird. Mark looked shocked. Just shocked. Then he said good-bye and hustled Brian away."

Mimi glanced at her watch. "We've got five minutes until the first bell, and I want to hear more about these dreams."

Karen had figured that was coming. There was no way she could tell Mimi about what had happened with Mark without at least mentioning the extent of her dreams. Of course, now Mimi wanted to hear the details. Karen made up her mind. It was all right. She needed to talk to somebody about how her nights had been influencing her days, and Mimi was her friend. "It may take a little more than five minutes."

Mimi frowned. "Are you stalling me?"

"No. But these aren't just regular dreams." Karen plunged in.

Now Mimi was intrigued. "I knew something was up with this dream stuff. When can we talk?"

"Can you come over after school?"

"I can't wait until then!"

"Mimi—"

"All right, all right. I can wait," she replied grumpily. She reached over and touched Karen's hair. "Has anyone said anything about your new look? Which, by the way, is already starting to turn into your old look."

Karen thought she had done a pretty good job of taking Mimi's handiwork and turning it into something that wouldn't scream, "Hey, I'm a makeover!" She had washed her hair a couple of times, and the henna rinse had faded to what she hoped was a healthy reddish glow. The hairdo itself looked nice, and Karen had turned down the makeup about fifty watts but had kept the lipstick and the mascara. "It's more me this way," Karen protested.

"I still think you need to have a little more dazzle if you want to get Mark's attention."

"Come on. Anything short of a blond and sleek

Jenny-Cullen-do isn't going to make it with Mark. Who cares anyway?"

Mimi didn't even bother to answer that. She just got up, grabbed her books, and said, "This afternoon. And the whole story this time, Karen, promise?"

Karen nodded. Mimi had to get to the other end of the school for her geometry class, but Karen's first period was one of her study halls, so she didn't rush. She thought she might go over her notes for the *Romeo and Juliet* test. Thank goodness, they were almost finished with the play. Ever since she had first heard them read in class, Mrs. Aikman had pegged Karen and Mark as the designated Romeo and Juliet readers. Karen didn't want to make one more speech declaring her love for Mark. "I mean Romeo," she mumbled. "Either of those jerks."

Feeling a little nervous about debuting her new look, Karen ducked into the bathroom so that she could look in the mirror one more time. As soon as she stepped inside, she knew she had made a big mistake.

"Oh, look who's here." Jenny Cullen turned to her best friend, Grace Ann Marko. Grace was ill-named and would have been out of Jenny's clique years ago if she hadn't been perfecting the art of toadying up to Jenny since the first grade.

Karen had an overpowering urge to run out of the bathroom, but she forced herself to walk calmly over to the mirror and pull out a comb.

"Do you think she's a natural redhead?" Jenny said in a loud whisper.

Grace giggled.

"I can appreciate why you think you needed a change, Karen," Jenny continued, "but slapping on a little makeup isn't going to get you someone like Mark Kennedy."

Karen looked at the girls' reflections in the mirror. "What's your problem, Jenny? Still worried that Mark might really have come back on Saturday night to see me?" She tried very hard to keep her voice even.

"He already told you—told both of us—he didn't."

Karen was sorely tempted to inform Jenny that Mark had told her just the opposite the next day, but she decided to let the opportunity go. Jenny would just think she was making it up anyway. "So then why the hostility? He's yours."

"I know." But Karen could see the uncertainty in her eyes. So Jenny did sense there was more to Mark and Karen's relationship than what was on the surface. And that's why she was spewing a little venom. This insight gave Karen confidence.

"Of course, you can't exactly be sure of that."

"Sure she can," Grace declared stoutly. "How could you think that someone as cool as Mark would like you?"

Well, that was plain enough, and Karen couldn't deny that to an unimaginative mind like Grace's, logic would dictate that Jenny and Mark would go together like coffee and cream or summer and sunshine. But just as Karen felt her momentary aplomb fading, she experienced a sensation so odd she had to steady herself at the bathroom sink.

Suddenly, the dirty tile walls and the stalls, even Jenny and Grace drifted away. For the space of a heartbeat, she was back in her dreams, sensing that Mark was so close she could touch him. Then she was back to reality, both trembling and feeling a powerful urge to laugh. Mark would die if he knew he had made an appearance in the girls' bathroom, even if it was just a psychic one.

"What's wrong with you?" Grace asked. "You're not going to faint or something, are you?"

"You do look a little strange," Jenny said, more coolly.

"I'm fine," Karen replied, and she was, actually. She dropped her comb back in her purse.

"You're out of your league, Karen," Jenny added, as Karen swung open the door.

"Or maybe you're out of yours." She wasn't sure if Jenny had heard her or not.

Karen managed to get through the day without seeing Mark until it was time for English class. To her surprise, considering that episode in the bathroom, she didn't even think much about him. It was as though that encounter, as strange as it was, had sealed something. She went about the rest of her day as if she was just an ordinary sophomore girl who didn't have weird dreams. She thoroughly enjoyed it.

By the time Karen arrived in Mrs. Aikman's room, she was in a good mood. She even gave Mark a pleasant hello. He responded with a suspicious, "Hi."

While the rest of the class filed in, Karen asked, in what she hoped was a casual tone, "So, did Brian say anything else about his dream yesterday?"

"What dream?" Mark asked sharply.

Oh, come on, Karen thought to herself. But she just leaned back and said, "Brian mentioned that he dreamed about us being friends."

"That's really all he said." Mark had been pretty freaked yesterday as he tried to quiz a silent Brian on the way home. Wasn't it bad enough that he had to spend his nights roaming through some Karen-tinged maze? Now, Brian was dreaming about her too?

Mark felt like being mean. "Haven't you got anything better to do than analyze the dreams of six-year-olds, Dr. Freud?"

Karen could have jumped on this remark, but all she did was smile. "Sometime we'll have to talk about dreams," she said boldly.

Mark just stared at her.

Mrs. Aikman came into the room, her arms full of tests. After greeting the class and brightly saying, "Test time!" she passed them out.

Karen breezed through the test. For Mark, it was a little more difficult, but he finished feeling fairly good about his answers. As he put the test on Mrs. Aikman's desk, he looked around to see if Karen was still anywhere around, but she had gone. Mark shook it off. He was supposed to meet Jenny outside anyway. There was no time for Karen even if she had been there.

Jenny was waiting outside, the top down on the black Honda that had been a gift for her sixteenth birthday.

"Hey," Mark said, suddenly getting a bright idea. "How about letting me drive?"

"You have your license?"

"Well, just a permit, but you're a licensed driver."

"My parents probably would say no. But they're not here," Jenny continued with a giggle. She slid over and let him take the wheel.

Mark didn't feel as confident driving with Jenny as he did with Rosanna. He was too conscious of making mistakes. His jerky exit out of the parking lot left him with a red face. He tried to make up for it by speeding down Central Street.

Jenny didn't seem to notice that he was going a little too fast.

"Did you see that Karen Genovese today?"

Mark took his eyes off the road for a moment. "What about her?"

"She's still trying to pull off that makeover she had on Saturday night."

"Hmm," was Mark's only comment.

"I saw her when she was in the bathroom this morning," Jenny continued. "You know, I think she has a crush on you."

"She said that?"

"No. Not exactly. But she gets this funny look on her face when she talks about you. She looked really weird in the bathroom."

Mark didn't know what to say to that. Why were they talking about him in the bathroom, anyway?

"You weren't lying to me were you?"

"About what?"

Jenny looked out the window. "You're not interested in her, are you?"

Was he going to lie again? Carefully, he chose his next words. "I barely know her, Jenny."

Jenny brightened. "I guess you don't. It's just that she acts like she's got this secret about you."

"Really?"

Jenny must have thought Mark looked a little too interested by the secret. She changed the subject. "Hey, did Bob Gilbert talk to you?"

Mark shook his head.

"He's the captain of the basketball team. He was saying that a couple of guys have moved and he wondered if you had ever played. Because you're so tall and all."

"I played a little in the city."

"He's really a great guy. He's going to talk to you about trying out. It would be awesome if you made the team."

Mark didn't know if he wanted to play basketball, but obviously it was important to Jenny.

"Pull into the Barn lot. There's a spot."

The lot was crowded, but Mark managed to squeeze the Honda between two cars. Casually, he threw his arm around Jenny as they walked into the Barn. People called out their names as soon as they stepped inside. Mark looked around and felt good. He was part of something here. This was real, not that stupid nighttime stuff. Why look for trouble? And Mark was pretty sure that's what Karen Genovese was—trouble.

"I'm going to the library," Gwen said as she grabbed a cookie out of the package on the counter.

"Are you going to ride your bike?"

"You sound like Barbara. Yes," Gwen mimicked her, "I'm going to ride my bike. I don't have any other way to get there."

Karen was relieved that Gwen was leaving. That way, she and Mimi would have the house totally to themselves. The last thing she needed was Gwen turning up at some inopportune moment and hearing something she wasn't supposed to.

Once Gwen was safely gone, Karen tidied up the living room a little and put the rest of the cookies out on a plate. Mimi had forgotten an afterschool dentist appointment, but she had promised Karen it wouldn't take long and she'd be over as soon as she possibly could.

Karen yawned as she stretched out on the couch. This lack of sleep was getting to her. Maybe she'd rest her eyes for a few minutes.

She didn't exactly fall asleep. And she didn't exactly dream. Karen was in that nether world where she was sure she was awake, but if she was, what were all those children in their odd-looking costumes doing in her living room? Brian, dressed like a superhero, was with them and they were playing but then they began looking at her on the couch, and she could tell that they wanted something from her. A frightened Brian held out his arms, as if he wanted to be picked up, but try as she might, she couldn't get off the couch. And she tried, and she tried—

"Karen!"

At first Karen thought it was Brian calling her, then she opened her eyes and saw Don looming over her.

"Oh, Don." She felt completely disoriented.

"Are you all right, hon?"

Karen sat up. "Sure."

"You were twitching and jerking."

"No, no, I'm fine. I must have drifted off."

Don sat down.

"What are you doing home so early?" Karen asked.

"I promised your mom I'd rake the leaves, and since I didn't have any more appointments this afternoon, I thought I'd get started."

"Yeah, there's a lot of leaves," Karen said dully.

Don cleared his throat. "Karen, Gwen told me you haven't been sleeping well."

Nice work, Gwen, Karen thought.

"Is something bothering you?"

"No," she said automatically.

"Well you know if there was you could come to me, right?"

Karen looked at Don's round, solemn face, and the force of several emotions hit her: sadness that her own father wasn't here to comfort her, and loneliness because she didn't feel she could confide in Don, and gratitude that he cared at all.

Karen reached over and patted his hand. "Thanks, Don."

Don seemed uncertain as to what to do next. He squeezed her hand and got up. "I'm going to change my clothes and then I'm going out to the yard."

"Mimi's coming over. We have some things we need to talk about."

"I won't get in the way of your girl talk."

Karen just nodded and watched him walk heavily out of the room. He was a nice man, but he wasn't Nick Genovese. Would she ever stop missing her dad?

Karen looked out the window and saw Mimi coming up the walk. She didn't wait for her to knock, but ran over and opened the door wide.

"That didn't take too long."

"It was only a teeth-cleaning." Mimi gave a fake smile. "Are they sparkling?"

"I'm glad you're here," Karen said, and was surprised to feel how true that was.

"I'm ready to listen if you're ready to talk."

"I guess I am." They grabbed some Cokes, and then Karen sat down on Don's recliner, across from the couch where Mimi had settled herself.

Mimi turned serious. "Why don't you start at the beginning and tell me everything, Karen."

"Everything? I'll tell you what I remember. That's always been the problem anyway."

Mimi waited expectantly.

"When I was a little kid," Karen began, "I had the same dreams, the same nightmares as everyone else. Monsters under the bed, witches, you know."

Mimi nodded.

"But then, when I was about five, the dreams started to change."

"How?"

"They were much more realistic. More real than real life."

"What were they about?" Mimi asked.

"They were about bad things that came true. First, my cat running away, then a doll being broken, and then . . ."

"Your father dying," Mimi finished for her.

Karen nodded, grateful not to have to say it. "I remember the first dreams, but I don't remember much about the dreams I had about my dad. I think I've blocked them out. I know I tried to tell my mother and my father that something was going to happen to him, but no one really paid attention to me. My mom kept trying to tell me that dreams didn't have any relation to what happened in real life."

"That turned out to be wrong."

"Very."

"Did you know how your father was going to die?" Mimi asked.

Karen picked at a small hole in her jeans. "That's the

part I don't remember. He died in a car crash. I'm not sure if it was the crash I dreamed about or just his death."

"What did your mother say about the dreams after he did die?" Mimi wanted to know. "She must have been totally freaked."

Karen shook her head. "It's funny, but I thought we never discussed it. Now my mom tells me she did ask me questions at the time, and I wouldn't answer. After that, we both tried to avoid the subject."

"Your dad dying," Mimi said, quietly. "Doesn't seem like it could get much worse."

"My mother was very upset when my dad died," Karen said carefully. She didn't want to seem like she was blaming her mom. "She wasn't herself for a long time. Till she married Don, really. That whole period is a blur for me. It was hard enough for both of us to cope with losing my father. I think we must have sensed that bringing my dreams into it would have made life even harder."

"So can't you talk to her about it now?"

Karen thought back to the interrupted conversation she'd had with her mother. "The subject scares my mother. It scares me."

"I can understand that," Mimi nodded. "And you must feel bad because you couldn't save him."

Karen looked at her, startled. It was the thought that had been playing around the edge of her conciousness for years, but she had never said the words out loud. "You're right. I do blame myself."

"You were just a little girl." Mimi continued gently. "Have you had other dreams come true? Lately I mean."

"I've had them all along, but nothing as important as the dream I had about my dad. When I was ten, I dreamed I was going to have my tonsils out, but my mother said I knew because I had overheard her talking to a neighbor."

"That could be," Mimi said, taking a sip of her soda.

"Does that explain how I knew the nurse's name and that my stepfather would give me a pink stuffed dog to cheer me up?"

"I'm impressed. But were the dreams *always* about something bad?"

"Not always. After my mother got engaged to Don, I knew we were going to move. I had the most vivid dream about this house. I had never seen it, but when we moved in, I knew the whole layout and what every room looked like."

"How often do you have these dreams?" Mimi wanted to know.

"It varies. I had gone a year or so without any before these dreams about Mark started."

At Mark's name, Mimi perked up. "I want to hear just what's happening with you and Mark in the middle of the night."

For the first time, Karen hesitated. This afternoon she thought she'd tell Mimi everything. But now, sitting here, Karen realized that some of the moments were just too private.

Mimi sensed Karen was holding back. "You promised," she wailed.

Karen made her decision quickly. There was still plenty to tell without confiding every detail. "I started dreaming about Mark before school started," Karen began. "The dreams were the virtual reality kind. Those are the ones that come true. I tried to tell myself it was all my imagination. Then, on the first day of school, Mark showed up at the bus stop."

"You must have died." Mimi put her hand over her mouth at her poor choice of words. "Oops. Sorry."

"Well, let's just say it freaked me out. Since then, I've had lots of dreams about Mark."

"Did they show trouble?" Mimi asked.

"Only in a vague kind of way. But now I'm dreaming about his little brother, Brian." Karen leaned forward. "I think Brian is in some kind of danger, or he's going to be."

"You don't know what kind of danger?"

"No. Not yet," Karen said grimly. "But now Mark and I are on the outs, so if I do figure out what's going on, he won't believe me." Karen looked at Mimi anxiously. "You believe me, don't you?"

"How can I not?" Mimi put down her drink, "Okay, okay. Let's think about this for a minute. You think something's going to happen to Brian. So the big question is, can you prevent it?"

Karen sat up straight. "I couldn't help my father. I was too little to do anything about the accident. But maybe these warnings will help me protect Brian." Her brave tone faded. "If only I can figure out what's going to happen—and what I'm supposed to do about it."

CHAPTER 9

Karen felt better after she had confided in Mimi, but she was surprised when the dreams stopped after that. Had just the act of telling another person about them made them disappear?

She couldn't deny that she was relieved to have the troublesome dreams gone, but mixed in with the relief was a profound sense of loss. She missed Mark at night, but sometimes Brian would drift around the edges of her sleep when she went to bed or first woke up. Thinking of Brian was always accompanied by a knot of worry in the pit of her stomach. Even without the dreams, she sensed the danger was still there.

At school, Mark was ignoring her now. They barely exchanged brief hellos during English class. Sometimes Karen got a glimpse of him in the center of a laughing crowd. Mimi had heard that he was trying out for the basketball team and passed that information back to Karen, who just shrugged.

As the days passed, Karen tried to tell herself that Mark was fading out of her life, just like the henna, which now added only the faintest of highlights to her hair. Without their nighttime meetings, Mark was just another boy in the popular crowd.

One evening at dinner, Mrs. Lewis said, "Have you made any arrangements with your grandmother yet? For your visit, I mean."

Karen looked at her mother sharply. "I thought you didn't want me to go."

"I never said that," Mrs. Lewis replied. "Not exactly."

"I haven't talked to her since she called."

Don poked around at his vegetable lasagna. "Weren't you excited about a weekend in New York?"

"It sounds like you guys want to get me out of the house."

"They just want to cheer you up," Gwen blurted out.

Boy, Karen thought, she must really be a lousy actress if she couldn't even fool this crew. Did she even want to go to New York now? The city itself was still a lure; her grandmother was less so. Somehow, seeing her grandmother had been tied up with the dreams and her father's death. Now none of it seemed very important.

"Maybe Mimi could go with me," Karen finally said. "Her dad and stepmother live in the city, and she goes in to visit them."

The thought of someone holding Karen's hand on the train into New York City perked up Mrs. Lewis. "Oh, that's a wonderful idea."

"Well, I'll run it by her," Karen said. "First, I guess, I should call Vivian."

After dinner, Karen looked up her grandmother's number. Before she could dial, the phone rang. A strange woman's voice was on the other end.

"Karen Genovese?"

"Yes."

"You don't know me, I mean, I was asked to call by Mr. Kennedy. I'm Brian's nanny, Rosanna."

Karen felt her stomach tighten. "Is something wrong?"

"Oh no," Rosanna laughed. "It's just that Mr. Kennedy wants to know if you can babysit for Brian on Friday night."

Karen didn't hear any voices urging her to go this time. No, now it was just her own desire, suddenly over-whelming, to see Mark out of school, perhaps alone, that made her answer, "I suppose so."

"Great! I would have had to give up one of my nights off if you hadn't said yes."

Well, she had done it now, Karen thought. Would Mark see this as the ploy that it was? For a few liberating seconds, Karen didn't care. Mark and Brian had drifted away from her, and now she had a ferocious feeling of wanting them back. What better place to see them than at their own house?

With a bit of renewed vigor, Karen dialed Vivian's number. She got the machine, but left a message saying she was available for a visit this coming weekend. She'd take the train down on Saturday and return on Sunday. Then Karen called Mimi to see if she wanted to go into the city, too.

"What a great idea," Mimi squealed. "I'll call my dad."

By the next day, everything was arranged. Karen and Mimi would go down in the morning; the girls would stay with their respective families but meet up for plenty of shopping. Karen hadn't talked to Vivian herself, but Don, who had taken her call, said Vivian sounded very happy that Karen could visit this weekend.

All that left was the babysitting to get through. When Friday night arrived, Karen was less enthusiastic about going. Her surge of desire had been momentary, but she didn't see any way out of the job. Even Mrs. Lewis said, "Wouldn't it be better if you stayed home to pack?"

"It's too late to get anyone to cover for me."

"Have you even decided what you're taking?" Mrs. Lewis fretted.

"Mom, I'm going to be gone exactly one night. I don't think I need to pack a trunk."

"Well, you don't want to walk into Vivian's looking like a ragamuffin."

So that was it. Karen remembered hearing from her mom about Vivian looking down her nose at the young Barbara. Apparently, her mother was concerned this disdain might continue into the second generation.

"I'll bring a dress, Mom."

"The blue one?"

"All right, the blue one."

Right now, she was more concerned about what she'd be wearing to Mark's house. It was cold enough for a sweater, so she wore a new one even though she had promised herself she would save it for a special occasion. Well, she could take it to New York as well. She wore the sweater with some faded jeans and threw on a jacket for the walk to the Kennedys.

It was Mark who opened the door. Karen hadn't been expecting that. "Hello," he said quietly.

Karen tried to smile.

Mr. Kennedy came into the hallway. "Come in, come in."

Mark opened the door wider and Karen came in. Mr. Kennedy waved her into the living room with the hand that was also holding his drink.

Feeling uncomfortable, Karen sat down on the couch. She could see Brian, already wearing his pj's, in the hallway. He gave her a plaintive wave.

"So, can I fix you something to drink?" Mr. Kennedy asked.

"Dad!"

Mr. Kennedy frowned. "I didn't mean anything alcoholic."

"No, I'm fine."

Mr. Kennedy freshened his own drink. "I'm sorry, dear, I've forgotten your name."

"Karen."

"Well, Karen, I've left the number where I'm going to be on the kitchen table." He said it almost triumphantly, as if to show Mark how responsible he was.

"Thank you."

"And I'll be back early, perhaps midnight or so."

Karen wondered when Mark was going to be back. And when he was going to leave, for that matter.

As it turned out, Mark and his father left at almost the same time. There was a honk, and Mark went flying out the door as though he were ten and the school bus was waiting. Mr. Kennedy was right behind him. "Get Brian in bed early, Karen," were his parting words.

Once they were gone, Brian finally made an appearance.

"Where have you been?" he asked accusingly.

"I guess you haven't needed a babysitter," Karen said carefully.

"I thought you were going to be here. When I needed you." He reached over and touched her hand.

"I didn't know you needed me," was all Karen could think to say.

Brian shrugged. Maybe it was because his father had left, but until it was time for bed, Brian shook off his melancholy and played like the little kid that he was. It was Ninja warriors again, and a short game of hide-and-seek. Karen was tempted to hide in Mark's room, but went into the laundry room instead.

Then it was Brian's bedtime. Karen made Brian brush his teeth and wash his face. As she was tucking him in, he said, "I hope I don't have one of those dreams again."

Karen immediately went on alert. "What dreams?"

Brian furrowed his brow. "The bad ones."

"What happens in them?"

"I don't remember, but it's bad."

Karen didn't want to press him. "Well, I'm here now, I'll protect you."

Brian snuggled under the covers. "I know."

The rest of the night passed uneventfully. Karen watched television, called Mimi to confirm their meeting at the train station, and tried to read. She half expected Mark to come back, the way he had the first night she babysat, but that didn't happen.

Precisely at midnight, Mr. Kennedy walked in. Karen had been worried that since he'd started the evening drinking, he'd finish it drunk, but he seemed to be all right when he came in.

"How did it go?" he asked.

"Fine," Karen replied, getting up. "Brian went to bed right on time."

"Well, let me run you home. I'm sure Brian will be all right for a few minutes."

Karen hated this part of babysitting. There was

nothing worse than trying to make conversation with fathers on the way home. At least this ride would be short.

Mr. Kennedy didn't need Karen's input to the conversation. He asked her if she watched *Bright Days* and barely heard her answer. He told her how important his job was, but that everyone else involved with the show was an idiot. He didn't mention either Mark or Brian. Karen couldn't remember the last time she had taken such an immediate dislike to anyone.

Everyone was asleep when she got home. Karen did a little more packing and then turned in herself. She thought she might toss and turn, considering the big weekend ahead of her. But she fell asleep immediately. And she dreamed.

There were no glass skyscrapers or even noisy lunchrooms in this dream. Karen was wandering alone down a dark road in a rainstorm, cold and miserable. She was looking for someone. At first, she didn't know who it was, but as the wind picked up speed and the rain beat down harder, she began running and realized it was Brian she needed to find. She called out his name, but the sound of her voice was carried away in the wind. Faster and faster Karen ran until she began to be sick with the very speed of her movement. She was rushing to meet something and the surge toward it terrified her.

A voice began moaning, "Oh no, oh no, oh no." The words picked up volume and began reverberating until

Karen didn't know whether they were inside her head or she was screaming along with them.

Finally, mercifully, the chant stopped. For a few seconds there was only the sound of silence. Then off in the distance, Karen heard a terrible crash. She thought it might be thunder, but she rushed on until, out of breath and sweating, she arrived at a clearing. A car, smashed and smoking, sat in the middle of the road like a crumpled cigarette hastily put out.

Alongside the automobile from which he'd been thrown lay an utterly motionless Brian.

CHAPTER 10

Karen woke up with her heart pounding. It took her a moment to realize where she was, and once she did, she buried herself under the covers.

She moved her head slightly so that she could see the clock radio glowing: 4:41 A.M. Brian's fine, she told herself. He hasn't gone out for a ride in the last four hours. He's home in his bed asleep. That he was safe—for now—was only a small comfort.

Tentatively, Karen sat up, trying to calm herself. Then it hit her. This wasn't the first time she had had a similar dream. Flooding back to her in a rush were the memories she had long suppressed: the terror, the voice, the crash. A body lying shockingly still. Then the body had been her father; now it was Brian.

What should I do? Karen wondered. She had told Mimi she wouldn't let anything happen to Brian. Would those just turn out to be empty words?

It took about an hour, an hour in which she fretted and tried unsuccessfully to figure out some plan, something that made sense, but finally Karen fell back into a dreamless sleep. When the alarm woke her at seven-thirty, she felt as if she had been drugged. The first picture that came to mind as she was shaking off her grogginess was that of Brian lying broken near the crumpled car.

Between her leaden head and her fear for Brian, the idea of going to New York seemed ridiculous, but Karen knew there was no way she could cancel the trip. Mimi would be waiting at the station, Vivian at her apartment. She had to go. Besides, what was the alternative? Just hanging around West Ridge for the rest of her life wasn't the answer.

Mrs. Lewis was in the kitchen having a cup of coffee when Karen got downstairs. "Packed? Ready?" she asked. "Do you want any breakfast?"

Karen was already grabbing some juice out of the fridge, and she took a bagel for the train ride. "This will be enough."

Mrs. Lewis sighed, but just got up and put her coffee cup in the sink. "Let's go then."

Karen didn't have to talk much on the ride to the train station. Her mother was full of advice about taking taxis and how to avoid panhandlers, and what to do if Vivian wasn't home.

"Why wouldn't she be home?" Karen said crossly. "She knows I'm coming."

"She knew yesterday," Mrs. Lewis said. "She has a tendency to forget things if something more interesting crosses her consciousness."

Karen just ignored that, and when her mother parked in the station lot, she practically flew from the car.

"Is Mimi here?" Mrs. Lewis called out the window.

"Uh-huh," Karen answered, although she didn't actually see her friend. "'Bye, Mom." Reluctantly, Mrs. Lewis pulled away.

Karen wandered into the train station, which was surprisingly full for a Saturday morning. Apparently, a lot of people wanted to spend their weekend in the city. Mimi was huddled in the corner on a bench. Karen thought she was sleeping like she did on the school bus, but Mimi opened her eyes as soon as Karen got close.

"What's wrong?" Karen asked. "You don't look so good."

"I don't feel very well," a pale Mimi admitted.

"Are you still going?" Karen felt panicky. She didn't want to be alone right now. Besides, she needed to tell Mimi about her dream and Brian.

Mimi sat up. "Sure. It's just a cold or something. I've got a headache, and my body feels achy."

"That sounds more like the flu."

"I'm not ruining our weekend," Mimi said in a more determined voice. "I'm sure I'll feel better once I get there."

Karen doubted that and felt selfish when she didn't suggest Mimi change her plans and go home. "Have you taken anything?"

"I just took some cold medication."

"Well, that's good. They've got orange juice in the machine over there." Karen popped up like a jack-in-the-box. "I'll go get you some."

By the time the girls boarded the train, Mimi was starting to look a little better. Karen decided she'd better plunge right in. "I had another dream, Mimi."

"Something bad?"

Karen nodded her head, then told Mimi all the awful details about Brian—and her dad. By the time she was finished, Karen felt as if she was the one coming down with the flu. At least, she felt shaky and ill.

Mimi sat up straighter. "You're sure this was like the dream you had about your dad? You told me before you didn't remember the details."

"I didn't—until now. But that body by the car, not moving . . ." Karen shuddered. "It was the same, I'm sure of it."

Mimi reached over and patted Karen's hand.

"Mimi, what am I going to do? Mr. Kennedy, he's not going to believe me. And Mark . . . well, I don't think Mark would understand either." Her Mark of the night might, but that boy had disappeared. The Mark that was at Jenny Cullen's beck and call probably wouldn't give her the time of day, much less listen to nocturnal predictions of doom.

"Then how can you save Brian?"

Karen felt a wave of relief in spite of herself. "So you think this all really means something. I'm not just going crazy?"

"How could I not take it seriously after what you told me before?" Mimi reassured her. "Besides, you're spooked, and you don't frighten easily."

"But what can I do about it?" Karen repeated, a desperate tone in her voice.

Mimi just shook her head. "I'm not sure. I wish I felt better, and could think more clearly."

Karen noticed beads of sweat on Mimi's forehead, though the train was not in the least bit warm. Karen sighed. She should have made Mimi go home. "Look, why don't you close your eyes. Get some rest. We can talk about this later."

Mimi nodded gratefully and closed her eyes. Karen, on the other hand, stewed all the way to New York. She just kept going over the same thing again and again. Brian was in danger of getting injured, even killed, and she could do nothing to stop it. The replay of her father's death, Karen pushed away altogether.

The train chugging into Grand Central Station jolted Mimi awake. Her face was flushed, and when Karen touched her forehead, it was hot.

"You've got a fever," Karen told her worriedly. "Is your dad going to meet you?"

"I think so," Mimi said in a small voice.

Karen was relieved to see Mr. Post waiting on the platform. He bundled Mimi off, but not before making sure that Karen got into a cab.

"I don't think Mimi will be going anywhere this weekend. Sorry, Karen," he said as he slammed the door.

Karen gave the cabbie her grandmother's address. The realization struck Karen that without Mimi as a diversion, she was going to have to spend the whole weekend with Vivian. Somehow that didn't seem even remotely possible. Determined not to think about Brian, for a while anyway, now Karen worried about her weekend. This visit was seeming like a very bad idea.

The cab pulled up in front of an elegant brownstone on the Upper West Side. Karen had vague memories of coming here when she was a little girl. Nervously, she paid the driver, overtipping so she wouldn't look like a hick, and climbed the stairs to the ivy-framed front door.

Expecting a maid to answer, Karen was surprised when Vivian opened the door wide. They both stood there awkwardly for a moment, neither of them making an effort to kiss. Finally, Vivian patted her on the shoulder and said, "Come in, come in."

There was nothing light and airy about the house, except, perhaps for the lace curtains at the living room windows. The couches were made of heavy wood and covered in a thick brocade. All around were antiques, but the kind that weren't very interesting, at least to Karen. "Oh, I remember that," she said, pointing to a large marble eagle that was perched on the mantel. "It scared me when I was little."

Vivian motioned her to sit down. "I'm sorry. I guess it might be frightening to a young girl."

There was another awkward silence, then Vivian asked, "Did you have a chance to eat before you left?"

"Just some juice." She never had gotten around to the bagel.

"Well, then, let's eat something. I had Josephine cut up some fruit and bring in pastries."

"Is Josephine still with you?" Karen asked with surprise.

"You remember her?"

Josephine was as old as the hills even back then, always looking at Karen as if she was about to break something. But all Karen said was, "Yes, I do."

"How nice. You must want to freshen up. Why don't you put that bag in your room, and I'll make sure the table is set." The brownstone had two floors, and Vivian brought Karen to a small room on the second floor that was decorated with the same dark colors and thick wood furnishings. Karen quickly did her little bit of unpacking and washed her hands in the tiny bathroom that was adjacent to the bedroom. Then she went downstairs to the dining room where the table was all laid out in beautiful flower-bordered china and silverware. Vivian was already sitting at the head of the table.

"It's so pretty," Karen said as she took her seat.

"You know it will all be yours someday."

Karen looked at her, startled.

"You are my only grandchild, after all." Vivian studied Karen. "Although, I must say you don't have much Genovese in you. You're Barbara through and through."

Karen certainly knew she didn't look much like her grandmother. She was already taller than Vivian, who was small-boned and petite in any case. Vivian's hair, piled on top of her head, was much darker than Karen's, and her style of dress could only be described as expensive. Several gold bracelets dangled from her grandmother's arm, and Karen was sure that the impressive diamond ring she was wearing was real. For just a moment she let herself wonder if that would be hers someday as well.

"How is Barbara?" Vivian continued. "I spoke with your stepfather."

"Mom's fine." Karen would have gone on, but Vivian didn't seem very interested.

"Good, good. Now, will you have tea or coffee? I presume you're too old for milk."

"Coffee with cream, please." Vivian poured and for a few moments they made idle conversation about the tastiness of the pastry and the freshness of the fruit. Then, abruptly, Vivian said, "You must wonder why I finally decided to get in touch."

"No. I mean, you *are* my grandmother."

Vivian's smile was thin. "It's very nice of you to leave it

at that. But as I said in my letter, I'm fully aware of what a dismal failure I must seem to you in that department."

Vivian's matter-of-fact tone made Karen more bold. "Well, I suppose a few birthday cards or letters at Christmas might have been nice."

Vivian nodded. "It wasn't you that I was avoiding. But I will tell you plainly, after Nick died, I couldn't seem to muster up much enthusiasm for his family. The memories were too harsh."

Karen tried not to let this hurt her feelings. But she did want to know more. "Memories of dad?"

"And his death. And, of course, your uncanny predictions about it."

Startled, Karen put down her cup. She had hoped that the dreams might come up in conversation, but she assumed that she would have to take some tortuous route to make that happen. Now, here was Vivian's casual mention of it with their visit less than an hour old.

"You know, uh, Vivian—"

"Does that feel more comfortable to you than Grandmother?"

"That's how you signed your letter."

"Yes. Well, I'm sorry I interrupted. What were you saying?"

"One reason I wanted to come here was to talk to you about that time."

Vivian lowered her eyes as she sipped her coffee. "Oh really. And why is that?"

"Because I don't remember everything that happened before my father died. And I need to."

"Your mother hasn't talked to you about those things?"

"Not a lot. It upsets her to think about the accident."

"It upsets me as well." Now Vivian's gaze was steady, "but I suppose I have no other choice. However, I don't want to discuss these things while we're eating. Very bad for the digestion. We can talk all you wish to later."

So Karen spent the next half hour or so introducing herself to her grandmother. Her life didn't sound very exciting even to her own ears. She tried to play up her good grades, but Vivian didn't seem particularly interested in her schoolwork.

"But who are your friends?" she asked, as she sipped her coffee.

"My best friend is named Mimi Post. She came in on the train with me. She's visiting her father."

"How about young men?"

"There's nobody special."

Vivian said, "Mmm," as if she knew the exact state of Karen's dismal social life. Then, abruptly, she asked, "Do you miss your father?"

"Of course I do."

"You remember him then?"

There was something about her grandmother's piercing gaze that made Karen answer honestly. "Not very well."

"Then how can you miss him?"

"I miss his . . . presence. Or maybe it's the idea of having a father that I miss."

Vivian nodded and stood. "I think I'm ready to talk now. Let's go to the living room where we'll be more comfortable."

It wasn't really more comfortable. The couches were stiff, as if no one had sat in them for a long time, but Karen tried to settle in.

"So," said Vivian, "since you don't remember Nicholas very well, let me tell you something about him. He was my only child, as you know. I had him rather late in life, and his father died when Nick was only eight."

"Not much older than I was," Karen murmured.

"He was a very bright boy and did well in school. Like you," Vivian acknowledged. "He was just finishing law school at Princeton University when he met your mother. She was also going to college in New Jersey, but not Princeton."

"No, it was a junior college."

"Yes. Well, they fell in love and they decided to get married. Without my permission, I might add. I tried to make the best of it. Barbara was nice," Vivian conceded, "and she did seem to love Nick very much. Of course, his career could have advanced much more quickly if he had decided to move back to New York, but he and Barbara wanted a small town." It was clear that this choice was inexplicable to Vivian, probably along with everything else Nick preferred.

"You came along in a year or so," Vivian continued, "and then I made it my business to try to get up to West Ridge more often."

"Did you?" Karen was surprised. She had almost no recollection of her grandmother visiting.

"Well, of course," Vivian said rather sharply. "As a matter of fact, I was staying with you when you began having those dreams. The house was small and you and I had to share a bedroom. You woke up, crying that something was going to happen to your father. Of course, we all tried to tell you you were just having bad dreams."

"That, I remember," Karen said quietly.

"I went home and didn't think much more about it," Vivian said. "After all, it is not so unusual for children to have nightmares. But the day before the accident, I came up again." Vivian looked off into space. "Perhaps I was having a premonition of my own. Certainly it was much too soon for another visit, but I wanted very much to see Nick, so I took the train up. I did get to see Nick before he left for a business dinner that evening. He never returned," she ended simply.

Vague recollections of that night floated through Karen's head. The wail of the police cars waking her up in the middle of the night, the commotion and the crying as Barbara and Vivian realized what had happened. Being left with a neighbor as they dashed to the hospital.

"But what about the dreams?" Karen persisted. "I knew it was going to be a car crash, didn't I?"

"Oh yes. You didn't seem to know the accident would be that evening, but when I was tucking you in, you told me, 'Daddy's car is going to crash.'"

Karen could feel herself start to shake. "Did I know anything else?"

"Yes. You knew it would happen because the driver was drunk."

CHAPTER 11

"I knew that?" Karen had absolutely no recollection of it.

"Well, you didn't explain it very well. You were quite young after all. But your meaning was clear."

"How did the accident happen?"

"It was a stormy night, and the car spun out of control. One of Nick's law partners, the driver, had been drinking. It was clearly established after the accident that alcohol was the cause."

"Was there anyone else in the car? Did they hit anyone?" Karen asked.

"No, it was just the two of them. They both died."

Vivian looked at her intently. "Tell me why this is all of such interest to you now, Karen."

Karen hesitated. She didn't really want to confide in her grandmother. She didn't know her well enough, and Karen wasn't too sure how she felt about all these weird goings-on herself.

When Karen didn't say anything, Vivian finally said, "Well, perhaps later."

"Yes," Karen replied gratefully. "Maybe in a little while."

"I began to tell you over brunch why I've been so anxious to see you, Karen." Vivian's gaze was piercing and she looked not unlike the marble eagle that looked down from the mantel.

Karen didn't say anything, almost afraid of what was coming next.

"As I implied, I have premonitions, too," Vivian said crisply. "They don't come in dreams like yours do, they are more like feelings. I have felt that something was going on with you, and it had to do with Nick's death. That's why I wanted you to come here, so we could talk."

The room, which had been overheated anyway, now became suffocating. Too much was happening in too short a space of time. Karen had to think about things, sort them through, but she couldn't do that here.

"Vivian, I told my friend Mimi I would meet her for lunch."

"What?"

Karen stood up. "I'm sorry, but she's waiting for me. Just a few blocks from here. She told me exactly where the restaurant was." Karen knew she was babbling, but she couldn't help it.

Vivian looked at Karen as if she understood everything, despite being told nothing. "Well, if you must go out, you must. You aren't very familiar with the city, but it is quite easy to find your way around."

"Yes, I know the cross streets and the rest are just numbers." Although anxious to get outside, Karen felt the need to reassure her grandmother. "I'll be back, soon, really. Then we can talk. About everything."

Vivian didn't walk her to the door, but Josephine was dusting silently in the hall. Karen nodded to her as she grabbed her jacket from the closet and practically flew outside.

Thank goodness the air was crisp, Karen thought to herself. It was the best thing for clearing her head. Although she had put on a confident face for Vivian, Karen wasn't very comfortable walking around, especially since she had no real destination. The streets were crowded, and while almost everyone seemed pretty normal, there were a few people who looked weird enough to make Karen keep moving at a brisk pace.

She thought she was leaving Vivian's to make sense of all that she had heard. But instead, she kept pushing those thoughts out of her mind. She glanced in store windows, and even went into one or two of the shops and rifled through racks of clothes. Finally she got tired and decided to find somewhere to sit and have another cup of coffee. Maybe she'd think about things then.

She had just crossed Columbus Avenue on the outlook for a cafe, when someone caught her eye. "It can't be," she murmured, but as she moved more quickly and caught up with the figure, she saw that she was right. It was Mark.

As if he sensed her presence, Mark turned around. "Karen!"

They stood there in the middle of the sidewalk, just looking at each other for a few seconds.

"What are you doing here?" Karen asked.

"I guess I could ask you the same thing," Mark said stiffly. "I came into the city to see some friends."

"I'm visiting my grandmother."

Neither of them spoke. The silence was becoming awkward when someone bumped into Karen, and Mark said, "We shouldn't just stand here."

"I was going to get a cup of coffee." Karen made herself ask, "Do you . . . do you want to come with me?"

Mark hesitated, then rather reluctantly said, "I guess."

They ducked into a nearby restaurant. Sitting alone together at a small table felt intimate, making Karen even more shy. They still had not exchanged more than a few bland sentences about the train and the weather when the coffee arrived.

There was so much Karen needed to say, but all she

could muster as an opening gambit was, "I can't believe I ran into you."

"It *is* kind of a coincidence."

Gathering up her courage, Karen said, "Maybe not. There's a lot I have to talk to you about, Mark."

Mark looked into Karen's eyes. He hadn't dreamed about her in a long time. In one way it was a relief, but he couldn't deny he had missed her. He had spent the last couple of weeks just filling time, keeping Jenny happy, which wasn't all that easy, or practicing for try-outs for the stupid basketball team that he didn't even want to be on. Now, sitting across from Karen, he was glad to see her, but nervous, too. Karen looked so serious. "What is it, Karen?" Mark finally asked. "Is something wrong?"

Well, there it was, her opening. Karen knew she should just begin talking, but instead, she had an almost overwhelming desire to get up, walk out of the restaurant, and never look back. No, this was her chance to do something to help Brian. Even if she looked liked an idiot, she had to at least try to explain to Mark the danger she thought his brother was in.

Karen took a breath. "Mark," she began intently, "what I'm going to tell you is very strange. I don't understand it myself, but it's true." Without pausing, without letting Mark say a word, Karen quickly told him the story of her father's death, and how she had foreseen his accident. She was about to tell him about Brian, but she couldn't quite yet. She asked him the same question she had put to Mimi. "Do you believe me so far?"

Mark had been listening quietly, sipping his coffee every now and then. "I wouldn't have believed you a couple of months ago. This all would have sounded like the way-out crazies. But lately, I've begun to think that maybe there is something to this dream stuff. I never could even remember my dreams, until I started dreaming about you."

Karen stared at him. "You've been dreaming about me," Karen repeated slowly.

"Sometimes they were in the lunchroom in school, and they've been in a city like Manhattan."

"Only cleaner," Karen murmured.

Now it was Mark's turn to stare. "How did you know?"

"I was there too."

Tentatively, tiptoeing around the more romantic parts, they began sharing bits and pieces of their dreams. Mark, too, had seen the sparkling river, even the children in their funny costumes.

Karen would have liked to linger trying to make sense of this all afternoon, but she hadn't gotten to the nightmare side of the dreams. It was time to talk about that now.

Mark smiled at her, that magnetic draw once again at work. Finally he said, "This is all new stuff to me, Karen. Do you know what it means?"

"I'm afraid I might."

Karen did look frightened. Without even thinking

about it he reached over and took her hand. It was freezing.

"Mark, I've been seeing someone else in my dreams."

"Who?"

"Brian."

Mark, too, had had disquieting moments in his sleep about Brian. And then, of course, there had been Brian's own restless nights. "Tell me," he said urgently.

Karen took a deep breath. "I didn't just dream about my father's death. I saw his body, crumpled next to a smashed-up car. Now I've been dreaming that Brian is in danger." Karen explained a little more as she watched Mark's face turn pale. She wanted to stop, but she forced herself to describe everything in just the detail she'd seen it, even down to Brian's broken body. Mark dropped her hand.

"I've scared you. I'm sorry."

"No, no. You had to tell me. I've had dreams about Brian, too, but they weren't clear. Karen, what are we going to do?"

"You don't know how many times I've asked myself that," Karen said desperately. "Maybe I'm wrong. No. I wish that was true, but I don't believe it. Something *is* going to happen."

"We can't take any chances," Mark said. He glanced at his watch. "I'm going to go home."

"I'm not saying you shouldn't, but what will you do when you get there? You can't watch Brian every second."

"That's what you think," Mark said grimly.

"There's got to be something more," Karen said. "Something we're missing. It's like a puzzle that we've got to figure out."

"Then we'll do that." Mark pulled out his wallet and left some money for the check. "Let me walk you back to your grandmother's. I'll still have plenty of time to make the next train."

They made their way back to Vivian's. Despite their fear about Brian, walking so closely, with the sun shining down on them, it was impossible not to feel happy about being together. When they got to Vivian's building, Mark said, "Let's walk around the block one more time."

Taking her hand again, Mark said, "Your father was killed by a drunk driver, right?"

Karen nodded.

"Then this must have something to do with my father. He's been drinking more and more lately."

"Can you talk to him?" Karen asked.

"Not really," Mark replied with a twisted smile.

"But if he thought he could hurt Brian . . ."

"He'd never believe this dream business. And no one tells my father what he can and can't do."

"Maybe you could call your mom. She'd be worried if she knew he was drinking and driving," Karen said.

"She's so far away," Mark murmured. Then, a little desperately, he added, "Somehow, I'll have to keep Brian away from my father, especially when he's had too much to drink."

"I'll take an early train in tomorrow." Karen tried to comfort him. "We'll have more time to figure it out."

"Oh no!"

"What?" Karen asked, alarmed.

"It's the Harvest Dance tonight. I have a date with Jenny."

"And you don't want to leave Brian."

Mark looked down on her. "That's part of it. Part of it is, I just don't feel like going out with Jenny tonight."

Karen reddened, hoping that meant what it sounded like. She had to add though, "It's kind of late to stand her up."

With a sigh, Mark said, "Yeah, she's been talking about this dance forever. Even though a dance is the last place I want to be, I guess it would be rude to call it off now."

"There's no reason to think anything bad will happen tonight," Karen said, trying to sound practical. "Who's going to be staying with Brian?"

"Rosanna. My father's going out. He's been going out a lot lately."

"Well, then, that should be all right. She's pretty good with Brian isn't she?"

"I guess. A little laid back, maybe, but Brian likes her okay."

"So, Brian should be safe tonight."

They were in front of Vivian's building again. For a minute, they just stood there looking at each other.

"Maybe your grandmother is watching out the window," Mark said.

"Maybe."

Mark touched her cheek. The feeling had all the electricity it had had in her dream.

Finally, they had to say good-bye. Karen, feeling a little like Juliet, drifted upstairs. Josephine, who opened the door, looked at her suspiciously. "Hello, Josephine," Karen said. "Where's my grandmother?"

"She's in her bedroom. She said to send you in as soon as you came back."

Vivian's room was the large one at the back of the second floor. To Karen's surprise the walls were covered with framed photographs of family. Vivian didn't seem like the sentimental type.

Vivian had taken off the wool suit she had worn for Karen's arrival and had put on a pretty dressing gown. She was lying down on the bed. "I'm sorry, at my age you need to rest, sometimes unexpectedly."

"It's all right," Karen said, sitting down at the edge of the bed.

Vivian looked at her shrewdly. "Something has happened. You practically glow with it. Why don't you tell me about your walk. And everything else, of course."

CHAPTER 12

Karen never would have believed it. How could a long-lost, mostly uninterested grandmother understand everything that was happening in Karen's life? And not just her real life, either. Vivian readily accepted that Karen could predict the future while asleep and meet her boyfriend in that shadow world as well.

Boyfriend. Karen didn't want to say the word, even to herself. But Vivian had thought it was perfectly natural to call Mark Karen's boyfriend. She listened avidly as Karen told her the whole story, leaving nothing out. Karen even mentioned how some of Brian's mannerisms reminded her of her father's. She watched her grandmother's face when she disclosed this, but its expression remained impassive.

When Karen was finally finished, almost spent with the effort, Vivian said, "It's up to you and your boyfriend, I think, to save his little brother."

Karen was taken aback. Vivian put it so boldly.

Vivian sat up a little higher on her bed. "As I've traveled the world, I've made it a practice to study other religions, other philosophies. The Western mind is the most practical, scientific. Other cultures are more attuned to the world of the spirit. Some believe in reincarnation, that souls can return in other bodies. Others believe that dreams can contain messages about the future. There are places on earth, Karen, where your dreams would not be considered strange at all."

A sense of relief came over Karen.

"But even if we are simply being practical, let's look at the facts." Vivian ticked off each one on her well-manicured fingers. "You dreamed your father was going to die in a car crash, and he did die in a car crash. You've seen other things, and they came true as well. Now, you are having nocturnal meetings with Mark, and he was dreaming the same things. Why shouldn't we expect something dire for Brian unless you stop it?"

"There's not enough to go on," Karen cried. "I don't know when, I don't know who."

Vivian considered this. "Let's go to the Met, shall we?"

"The Met?" Karen asked with confusion.

"The Metropolitan Museum of Art. It's not far from here, and it's quite fabulous. I often go and look at the paintings when I want to clear my mind."

"Well, if that's what you'd like . . ." This was hardly what Karen had expected.

Vivian patted Karen's hand. "Indulge me. I promise you, this little excursion will get us closer to a solution, not further away."

Karen got up off the side of the bed. "I'll wait downstairs while you get dressed."

"Karen."

"Yes, Vivian?"

"Your dreams weren't enough to save your father. Perhaps this is the universe's way to have the same scenario play out with a better ending."

"You really think so?" Karen asked hopefully.

"Don't worry. I cannot believe you were given all this information without also being given a way to help."

It was something to hold on to, Karen thought as she headed downstairs. She chewed on her fingernail. But there had to be some way to find out more.

If she hadn't had more pressing things on her mind, Karen would have adored the Met. The stone building was impressive itself from its massive stairs to the winding hushed halls where masterpieces waited to be seen.

As they wandered the galleries, Vivian seemed to have forgotten all about auto accidents, Mark, and even Brian. She visited some of her favorite paintings, introduced Karen to them, and insisted they go to the special exhibit of ballgowns in the costume collection.

"There's one that would look divine on you," Vivian said, pointing to a sea-green dress of fluff and foam encrusted with jewels.

"I have no place to wear it, Vivian," Karen said with a smile. "I don't think anyone does."

Vivian shrugged sadly. "I suppose you're right. Not anymore."

It felt good, though, that Vivian could see her in such a dress. As they walked along, Karen daydreamed about wearing it while dancing with Mark.

Every so often, Karen glanced over at her grandmother to see if Vivian was working on the problem of Brian's safety, but Vivian seemed maddeningly serene. Karen waited until they were outside once more, but then, she could contain herself no longer. "You said the museum could clear your mind. Has it?"

"Oh, it's very clear, but no ideas have filled it yet."

"But Vivian . . ."

"Shall we stop for some hot chocolate?"

Karen almost stamped her foot. "This isn't getting us anywhere. Vivian, are you listening to me?"

Dusk was slowly falling. Vivian was staring across the street, as if she could not quite make something out. "Karen, what are those two people dressed up as?"

Karen glanced in the direction her grandmother was

pointing. "She's Snow White and he's one of the dwarfs, I guess."

"But why are they in costume?"

Karen shrugged. "It's the Saturday before Halloween. They're probably going to a party."

Vivian's brow furrowed. "Halloween," she murmured.

Vivian had been out of the country for a while, but surely she remembered what Halloween was.

"You said that in some of your dreams, people were wearing costumes, didn't you?" Vivian asked.

"Yes, sometimes. Mark said he dreamed about children in costumes, too. But the costumes never seemed all that important."

Vivan clutched Karen's hand. "I think they are. Do you know when your father died?"

"I know it was in the fall. But Mom never liked to remember the date."

Vivian looked up at her. "It was also the weekend before Halloween. Not the same date as today, mind you, but it was late Saturday night or early Sunday morning."

"The anniversary of the car crash!" The look of realization on Karen's face turned to dread. "Vivian, we have to get back to West Ridge."

Vivian began walking briskly. "Yes. I'm afraid whatever is going to happen, it will be tonight."

A shaking Karen said, "Vivian we should stop and call Mark."

"Let's do that," Vivian agreed. "Then we will call the station and find out about the next train."

"Can't we drive?"

"Drive what?" Vivian said. "I don't have a car. Most people don't in New York City."

"Oh, of course, of course," Karen said distractedly. They ducked into a hotel whose lobby was almost as ornate as Vivian's apartment. Karen would have been too intimidated to ask the location of a phone, but the doorman almost bowed and scraped when Vivian asked him. In an old-fashioned phone booth, Karen picked up the receiver and then realized she had no idea what Mark's phone number was. Even though her head was pounding, she managed to call information in West Ridge, only to find the number was unlisted.

Vivian tried to calm Karen down. "We'll get him somehow," she comforted her granddaughter. "Let me check on the train now."

As it turned out, there was a train leaving shortly. Karen and Vivian practically had to fly out of the hotel to grab a taxi.

Vivian was breathing heavily as she leaned back against the cab seat.

"Are you all right?" Karen asked with concern.

"Fine, fine. I'm just not used to moving so quickly."

"Maybe you shouldn't come back with me. Just get me on the train, and you can go home."

Vivian waved Karen's concern away. "Don't be silly.

Let you worry alone all the way to West Ridge? Of course not. Besides, perhaps we can figure out more on the ride back."

When they arrived at the station, Karen wanted to try Mark one more time; she was even willing to call Jenny and get the number, but there wasn't any time. They had only moments to find the proper track and board the train.

"Oh, dear," Vivian said as the conductor helped her get on the train. "I wonder what Josephine will think when I don't return."

"We'll call her, too, as soon as we can."

As they rode along, Karen and Vivian tried to go over what they'd figured out.

"So it seems the accident will happen tonight, because the weekend before Halloween is when it happened before."

"I believe that is the missing piece of the puzzle," Vivian replied. "I think that's why your dream last night was so intense."

"Then there must be a change in Mr. Kennedy's plans," Karen said thoughtfully.

"The boys' father? Why?"

"Didn't I tell you? Mark and I think he will be the driver. He's the one who drinks too much, just like the man who was my father's partner."

Vivian looked at Karen oddly. "I never said the person with your father that night was a man."

"Well, I just assumed . . ."

"No, not at all. It was a woman."

"But Mark thinks Brian is safe tonight because his father will be away for the evening," Karen said, her voice rising.

"Who will the boy be with tonight?"

"His babysitter. Rosanna."

CHAPTER 13

Once he arrived home, Mark would have liked nothing better than to go to bed and sleep for hours—and not just because he might dream about Karen. This day had been almost too much for him. Even during the train ride, when he'd done nothing but stare out the window and think, there hadn't been enough time for him to get everything straight.

First he had thought about Karen and the incredible knowledge that their meetings had been a mutual event, not a solitary nocturnal roaming. He wanted to relive both his night life and his real life, but he found it difficult to keep his mind on Karen for very long. Brian's face kept intruding.

Then all thoughts were of his brother. How could he make sure that nothing would happen to Brian? If he tried to keep him out of cars, his father, Rosanna, even Brian would probably protest. Yet to do nothing—well, that could be disastrous.

As he watched the hilly countryside from the train window, Mark's thoughts shifted to his father. His father had always been temperamental and calmed himself with liquor, but never as much as he'd been doing lately. The connection between Mr. Kennedy's drinking and Karen's dream made Mark shudder, and he thought about calling his mother. Maybe there was some way that she could send for Brian.

And then, when there was just a crack of empty space to let in a spare thought, Mark had to spend a moment on the Harvest Dance. God, he didn't want to go. No matter what he'd decided in New York, he was seriously considering calling Jenny and telling her he couldn't make it. That was such an unpleasant prospect that he went back to daydreaming about Karen.

When he reached the train station, Mark knew that he could call Rosanna to pick him up, but he was so anxious to get home, he decided to just make the mile walk himself. The last quarter mile, he sprinted.

"Anybody home?" he called as he opened the door.

The house was silent, but there was a strong and familiar smell coming from the back. Mark followed the aroma to Rosanna's room at the back of the house. He called out her name.

It was a red-faced—and red-eyed—Rosanna, who opened her bedroom door. "What are you doing back?"

"I guess I don't have to ask what *you're* doing." Mark could clearly see the marijuana joint burning in the ashtray.

"Oops. Sorry," Rosanna said with a lopsided grin. "But don't tell your dad, okay?"

Mark looked at Rosanna with anger. She was supposed to be taking care of Brian. How many times had she done her job while stoned? "Where is my dad?" Mark asked without answering her questions. "Where's Brian?"

"Your father had errands. Brian went with him."

Mark swore to himself. Brian hardly ever went with his father. Why did he have to start going now, of all times? Still, his father rarely drank in the daytime. It was probably safe for Brian to be out with him now. Was this how he was going to be now? Terrified every time Brian was out of his sight?

Marching back to his room, Mark was struck by another terrible thought. Rosanna spent a lot of her time driving Brian around. Was she ever at the wheel when she was high on grass? Maybe it wasn't Mr. Kennedy who was the danger to Brian at all. Maybe it was Rosanna.

Mark slammed his door and flopped down on his bed. He was beginning to feel as if he was in a very bad movie. When the phone rang, he didn't even reach over to answer it, but then he thought perhaps it was Karen, and he picked up.

"So are you getting ready?" a voice bubbled in response to his hello.

"Jenny?"

"Of course. Who else would want to know if you were getting ready for the dance?"

"Well, Jenny, I've sort of run into a problem with the dance," Mark said, tentatively. Maybe he could ease into this.

"Why?"

"Jenny, there's some trouble at home. I might not be able to go."

"Oh, Mark, no!" Jenny wailed.

Mark immediately felt guilty.

"This is the biggest dance of the year. I've got a new dress." She sounded like she was about to cry. "I'll miss everything."

"I only said might," Mark said lamely.

"What's wrong, anyway?"

Knowing there was no way he could explain, not then, not ever, Mark just said, "It's complicated. Family stuff."

"But when will you know for sure?"

He had been right the first time. Standing Jenny up at this late date wouldn't serve any purpose. It wasn't as if there was any reason to think something was going to happen to Brian this particular evening.

Mark sighed. "Jenny, don't worry about it. Whatever else happens, I'll be there."

"You will?" She sounded happy and relieved.

"Yeah. Seven. I'll be there."

A half hour or so later, Brian and his father came home. Mark breathed a sigh of relief. He went over and gave Brian a small hug, but the boy shook him off.

"Where did you go?" Mark asked.

"We went to the hardware store," Brian answered in a flat voice.

"Brian wasn't a very good boy," Mr. Kennedy added as he poured himself a drink.

"It was an accident," Brian protested.

"He was running around the store and practically knocked down a woman."

Brian hung his head.

"Say," Mr. Kennedy asked, "what was the name of that girl who babysits for Brian?"

"Karen. Why?"

"Do you think she might be free tonight?"

"She's in New York, visiting her grandmother."

Mr. Kennedy shook his head. "It's probably too late to get someone else. Rosanna was supposed to sit, but now she wants to go out. I suppose I'll just tell her she has to stay."

Mark was feeling uneasy. "Maybe you could cancel your plans." Mark wished everybody would stay home, safe.

"The producer of the show called. He wants to have dinner. It's a command performance," Mr. Kennedy said grimly.

"Mark, can't you stay home with me?" Brian asked plaintively.

Mark went over to Brian and patted him on the shoulder. "You remember I told you there's a dance tonight? Jenny would be really upset if I didn't go."

"I don't like her, anyway," Brian pouted.

Jenny had come home with Mark a couple of times after school, and Brian had taken an immediate dislike to her. Mark had figured it was just because he was so fond of Karen, but whatever the reason, Brian made it a point to go into his room and slam the door whenever Jenny was around.

"I know, sport, sorry about that, but it still wouldn't be very nice of me not to show up."

Brian shrugged and went to his room.

"Brian is getting very hard to handle," Mr. Kennedy grumbled, as soon as Brian was out of earshot.

"I think he's a pretty great kid," Mark said boldly.

Mr. Kennedy flopped down on the couch. "Oh, that's easy for you to say. You're just the brother."

Mark asked a question that had been on his mind ever since they had left California, but one he'd always been too afraid to say out loud. "Why did you take us with you, Dad? Why didn't you just leave us with Mom?"

Mr. Kennedy looked at him steadily. "We told you. We thought it would be better for everybody."

"What does that mean?"

"Frankly, Mark, it means that your mother has never quite been able to decide whether she wants to be married to me or not." Mr. Kennedy took a swig of his drink.

"And I didn't want to leave you guys with her while she was making up her mind."

"She didn't want us with her?" Mark asked, stricken.

"Oh, she wants you," Mr. Kennedy said bitterly. "It's me she isn't too sure about. But you know how your mother is, flighty, not very big on details. The idea of keeping you boys with her was more appealing than the actual work it would have involved. I said it would be better for you guys if you came with me."

Mark was shocked, but tried not to show it. He always thought of his mother as the "good" one. "And she agreed?"

"You forget, when we left California, I had a steady job. Your mother was off making that TV movie in Bali. She's back on a soap now, but then taking care of you would have been a problem. She had to be available for auditions or going on shoots, or for that matter, going on dates."

Dates? His mother was going on dates? "Well, thanks for telling me," Mark said uncertainly. This was one more bit of difficult news for him to assimilate.

"Mark," Mr. Kennedy said, in a softer tone of voice, "I know I seem like a bear sometimes, but it's not easy being a single parent. And now that things are all screwed up at work . . ." He took another gulp of his drink. "It's not easy, that's all."

Mark nodded. He almost felt sorry for his dad. And he felt stupid. "I never really thought about you and Mom not getting along. We've all gone back to California together to see her, and she's come to New York . . ."

"Not in a while."

"No, not all together. But when we have been together, you two seemed fine."

Mr. Kennedy smiled grimly. "Your mom's an actress, and I know a little about acting myself, don't forget."

"Are you and Mom . . . ?"

Mr. Kennedy sighed. "I haven't got a clue."

"Oh." Mark watched his father get up and pour a little more liquor into his drink. He could feel the terror rising inside him. "Dad, the drinking . . ."

"What about it?"

"You've been drinking more than usual." Mark felt a little sick at talking to his father like this, but he felt he had to try.

"So?" Mr. Kennedy asked, belligerent once more. "Aren't I entitled to a relaxing drink when I get home?"

This was going nowhere, Mark thought. Maybe he could catch his father when he was in a better mood. "I'm gonna get ready for the dance now."

"Fine. Have a good time." His father lifted his glass in Mark's direction.

Mark felt terrible as he got dressed. Everything was closing in on him. His parents were probably splitting up, and he didn't know how to protect Brian. He reached for the phone several times to call Jenny and tell her he couldn't go, but reminded himself how futile that was. What was he going to do, quit school and spend his life protecting Brian? Besides, he wanted to, needed to get away from the millions of thoughts swarming through his head like bees let out of a hive. Even going to this stupid dance with a girl he didn't want to be with was better than staying home and thinking.

When he was ready to leave, he stopped at Rosanna's door. She was watching a home shopping channel on the small TV by her bedside. She still looked pretty blissful.

"Oh, Mark," she said, starting when she finally noticed him. "Hey, man, you're looking good."

"Thanks," Mark said shortly. "What are your plans for tonight?"

Rosanna looked at him blankly. "You know, I tried to get out of sitting but it was too late."

"So you're going to stay home."

"I don't have a choice."

Mark felt marginally better. "And you're not going to smoke dope when you take care of Brian, are you? I mean, I could bust you with my dad, anytime I even think you're smoking."

"I don't smoke when I'm responsible for Brian."

Mark wasn't at all sure he believed her, but at least she looked worried. It would have to do for now. Later, he decided, he would tell his father.

Despite all his apprehensions, Mark showed up at Jenny's door right on time. He had to admit she looked pretty great, too. The wine-colored velvet dress she was wearing seemed molded to her body. If Karen hadn't been in the back of his mind, he might have been a goner.

It was a little embarrassing to have Jenny drive to the dance, but she didn't seem to mind. "Maybe if you're a good boy, I'll let you get behind the wheel later," she teased him.

"Okay," Mark said, although he wished he were the one driving up to the high school.

Jenny had groused about the dance being held in the gym, but even she had to admit the decorations committee had done a terrific job of decorating the place. Scarecrows and paper haystacks did a lot to hide the usual gym equipment, and everyone looking their best helped, too.

Still, Mark couldn't really get into the swing of the evening. It didn't take long for Jenny to notice.

"You're no fun," she said, after he mindlessly danced her around the floor for the second time.

"I told you I had family things going on."

"Well, maybe you should call home, then."

Jenny meant it sarcastically, but Mark thought that was an excellent idea. When the music stopped, Jenny gave Mark a withering look and headed outside where several of the kids in her crowd were gathered together, laughing and talking.

"How are you, Bri?" Mark said when his brother answered.

"I'm okay."

"Did Dad go out?"

"Yeah."

"All right, well I'll be home as soon as I can. Go to sleep soon."

"I will. Oh, Mark. Right after you left, Karen called."

"Karen?" Mark's mind whirled. She knew he was at the dance. "What did she say?"

"She said to tell you two things if you called."

Mark waited patiently while Brian tried to remember the message. "She said, the driver is a woman."

"A woman!"

"And . . . and . . ." Brian faltered, trying to get Karen's words straight.

"What, Bri, tell me," Mark implored.

"It's happening tonight."

This is how it must feel to be drowning, Mark thought as he hurried back into the gym after his phone call to Brian. He couldn't catch his breath, and he was going under for the third time.

He didn't know how Karen had figured out that the crash would be tonight, but if the driver was a woman, it must mean Rosanna. If only he'd told his father about the dope. But he hadn't, and if Karen was right and the danger was this evening, Mark knew he had to get Brian away from Rosanna as fast as possible.

Scanning the gym, Mark looked everywhere for Jenny, but she was nowhere to be seen. He pushed his way through the dancing couples once more, trying to find her, until finally, he spotted her still outside, slightly obscured by her gang of friends. As Mark hurried up to her, he noticed that her whole mood had changed. She seemed to be having a great time now. Her eyes were bright, her cheeks flushed, and she was laughing up at a couple of the senior boys.

"Jenny, I have to talk to you."

She frowned. "Why? Is your phone call finished?"

"Please," he said. She was his best chance of getting home as soon as possible.

"Okay." She shrugged.

He pulled her off to the side of the gym. "Look, I need your help."

"For what?"

"My brother. He's . . . he's in trouble."

Jenny looked like she wasn't taking this all in.

"It's important that I get home, right now. His babysitter, well, I think she might hurt him. We have to get him out of the house." He knew he sounded a little hysterical, but that's how he felt.

"So we have to leave now?" Jenny was getting it, and she wasn't happy.

"Okay, fine, stay. I'll get home some other way." Mark turned away.

"No, no. If he's in trouble . . ."

Mark was halfway out to the parking lot, barely noticing Jenny stumbling to keep up.

"Do you want to drive?" Jenny asked.

For once in his life, Mark didn't, but Jenny was holding out the keys, so he grabbed them and got behind the wheel. It had started to rain, and the roads were getting a little slick. Mark tried to relax, but between the wet conditions and his nerves, it wasn't easy. When Jenny tried to speak, he told her he needed to concentrate. Driving down his dark street, Mark noticed that most of the lights in his house were off. His stomach flipped over. "The van's not in the driveway."

"They're gone?" Jenny asked.

Mark jumped out of the car and unlocked the door to the house. He called out for Brian and Rosanna, but it was clear no one was home. In a few seconds he was back in the car. "We have to find them," Mark said, his voice shaking. He gunned it out of the driveway.

"We can't just ride around," Jenny said nervously. "They could be anywhere."

"Maybe I should go to the police station."

"Not the police," Jenny exclaimed.

Before he could ask her why not, Mark caught sight of a van that looked like the Kennedys' parked in the lot of the convenience store. Jenny gasped as he made a sharp left into the parking lot.

Almost immediately, Mark spotted Rosanna and Brian coming out of the store. He jumped out of the car and raced over to them. "Where have you been?" Mark asked, fury in his voice.

Rosanna looked at Mark as if he was crazy. "What are you doing here?"

Brian, who was wearing a heavy sweater over his pajamas looked as if he'd been crying. Mark pulled Brian toward him. "What did you do to him?" he yelled at Rosanna.

"Nothing."

Brian reached up for Mark to pick him up. "She made me go out. In the rain."

"Look, I needed cigarettes, and Brian wanted candy—"

"But I didn't want to go out," Brian interrupted.

"Mark, all I did was—"

"It doesn't matter," Mark said, shifting Brian in his arms. "I'm taking him with me."

"I can take him home," Rosanna objected.

"Over my dead body!" He turned away from Roseanna and headed to the car. Mark tried to put Brian in the front seat with Jenny, but Brian just held on to him more tightly.

"I don't want to go with her," Brian cried.

"We have to." But Brian refused to sit next to Jenny.

"You drive," Mark ordered Jenny curtly. "I'll sit with Brian."

Jenny looked as if things were happening way too fast for her, but she moved over into the driver's seat. "Where am I going?" Jenny asked.

He didn't want to have another ugly scene with Rosanna back at the house, at least not immediately. "Just drive."

The rain started falling harder, and so did Brian's tears. He sat on Mark's lap and buried his head in his brother's shoulder.

They wheeled by Karen's house. An urge to stop grabbed Mark, but that was stupid. She was in New York.

By the time the sensation had passed, Mark realized something. "You're going too fast, Jen," Mark told her. "Slow down."

"All right," she muttered, but Jenny was having trouble controlling the car in the pounding rain. She began swerving raggedly down the street through the great puddles of water that blocked the road. Brian's silent tears turned into a wail.

"Pull over!" Mark demanded, but Jenny seemed not to hear. The car suddenly picked up speed as if Jenny had put her foot on the gas instead of the brake. Then, in the middle of the road, like an apparition, a girl appeared.

"Don't you see her?" Mark yelled. "It's Karen. Stop, Jenny!"

Agonizingly, with a squeal of the brakes, the car skidded and twisted to a stop, causing Brian to cry even harder. Mark rolled down his window. "Karen! I've got him."

Karen peered into the car. When she saw who was driving, her face paled. "So it was Jenny."

Karen held on to Mark's hand. It felt good to be out walking together without any threats hanging over their heads.

"It was good to see my mom and my grandmother sitting around the breakfast table together this morning," Karen said, "but I needed to get out of the house."

"Too many questions?" Mark asked.

Karen nodded. "I think I'll let Vivian answer them for a while."

"Don't think I didn't have to answer a few myself last night."

Karen glanced around at the nice houses, the well-manicured lawns. Everything looked so normal, it was hard to believe that last night had happened at all. "Did your dad believe any of it?"

"I think he's too stunned to be sure. Rosanna was furious by the time Brian and I got home. I think she was ready to call the police. So when my dad got back, there I was, trying to calm down Rosanna *and* Brian."

They came to a small children's park and sat down on one of the benches. "It's funny," Mark continued, "but last night of all nights, I don't think he'd been drinking at all. I put Brian to bed, and Rosanna stomped off, and then I told my dad what had happened. I said I'd even bring you and Vivian over today to explain it again. He just kept shaking his head. Finally I told him I was going to bed, and after I turned off the light, he did the weirdest thing."

"What?"

"He came and stood in the doorway like he used to do when I was a kid and said, 'Good night Marco Polo.' That's what he used to call me when I was Bri's age. He hasn't done that in about a million years."

"Have you seen him this morning?"

"No, no one in my house is up yet. But I have some questions for you."

Karen leaned back and looked up at the sky. "Go ahead."

"How did you get out in the road? How did you know we'd be driving by there?"

"Let me go back a little. When we were on the train, and Vivian told me the driver that night had been a woman, I freaked. I said I had to call you right away, and I was ready to pull the emergency brake on the train if I had to."

Mark looked at her with admiration. "Wow!"

"But I didn't have to. You should have seen Vivian. She understood the situation instantly, and then very politely asked a man who she'd seen using his cell phone if she could borrow it for an emergency."

"But how did you get the number?"

Karen, a little embarrassed, said, "Well, I remembered I had your number at home. In my room."

"Near your bed," Mark teased.

Karen ignored that. "So I called home and had Gwen find it. Then I called your house."

"Why didn't you talk to Rosanna?"

"She was taking a bath, and I couldn't keep the phone forever. The man was already giving us dirty looks. So I just gave Brian the message and hoped you'd call."

"Okay, so then you got home," Mark prompted.

"And I knew you must have already left for the dance."

"Weren't your parents shocked to see you?"

"And Vivian." Karen could smile about it now, but last night, when so many things were happening at once, it had been hard to separate one odd reality from another.

Karen had been almost hysterical as she'd told her parents she had to get to the gym. Don, to her everlasting gratitude, hadn't even bothered to find out the whole story but had bundled her into the car and headed off to the high school.

"Poor Don, I was trying to tell him what happened, and I don't think any of it was making much sense. As soon as we pulled into the parking lot, I ran out of the car. It was pouring by then, and I walked into the biggest dance of the year looking like a wet washrag."

Mark put his arm around her and drew her close.

"Naturally, the first person I saw was Grace, and she stared at me, maybe because I looked so awful or because I just kept asking everyone where you and Jenny were. Finally, when I let her get a word in edgewise, she said the two of you had gone back to your house. Family emergency. So I came back to the car frantic and told Don to drive me to your house. When we were heading down St. John's Road, I got that strange feeling, just like the one I had in the girl's bathroom that day." Karen looked at Mark. "Reality just kind of shifted for me, and I knew that your car would be coming by there any minute and the car would crash if I didn't stop you. So I had Don pull over, and I ran out of the car, and well, you know the rest."

Mark murmured softly, "You saved us." After a moment he said, "If only I'd have been smarter, it wouldn't have gone so far. There I was hustling Brian into a car when it was the one thing he was supposed to stay away from."

"You had to get him home somehow, and you thought he'd be safe with you."

"I never gave the car two seconds' thought. I just wanted to get him away from Rosanna. Instead we got into a car with a drunk driver."

"You didn't know Jenny had been drinking with her friends?"

"I should have realized something was up when she didn't want to drive, but I was too crazed to notice." Mark's laugh was short and harsh. "I guess it's true what they say about vodka. You can't smell it on a person's breath."

"She felt pretty bad when it was over," Karen said quietly.

"I think she'll be pretty glad to be rid of me."

"You know, there's going to be a lot more questions in school on Monday." She thought about what a story this was going to make for Mimi.

"I'm not so sure," Mark replied. "I don't think Jenny will want anyone to know that she almost had an accident while she was driving drunk. And even if people do ask questions, we don't have to answer."

Karen felt lighter than she had in years. "It's finished something for me. I feel, I don't know, free."

"I guess that's another part of the miracle, like everything else that's happened to us."

"Miracle. That's a good word for it." Karen wondered if maybe her father knew about the miracle, too. Maybe he did.

"Now all we need to do is be together and have fun." Mark's sigh was full of relief. "Finally."

"Until you go to California for Thanksgiving," Karen reminded him. "I'm going to miss you."

"It will only be for a couple of days."

"Right now, that sounds like a long time to not see each other."

"Not see each other? What are you talking about?" Mark smiled down at her. "I'll see you in my dreams."

ILENE COOPER, a former children's and young adult librarian, is the author of several popular series for young adults, including *Hollywood Wars* and *The Kids from Kennedy Middle School,* and the novel *Buddy Love Now on Video.* Among her series for middle-grade readers are the books about *The Holiday Five.* She lives in Highland Park, Illinois.